Shadows

of the

Heart

Aditi. J

Copyright © 2025 Aditi. J

All Rights Reserved.

Made with ❤ on the Notion Press Platform

www.notionpress.com

To my family,

Who always stand by my side.

To everyone who believes in 'one more chance'.

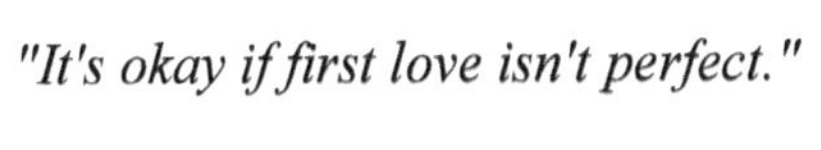

"It's okay if first love isn't perfect."

In a world where trust is a weakness,

and love is a weapon,

they were bound to collide.

Both scarred by their pasts,

their hearts guarded like fortresses.

But even in the darkest of nights,

a spark can light a fire.

1

Adrian

I sat in the dimly lit bar, swirling the ice in my glass, lost in thought. The room was filled with the low murmur of conversation, the clinking of glasses, and the faint scent of stale cigarettes. It was the kind of place where people went to forget—fitting, considering how hard I'd been trying to do just that. But no matter how much I tried, the memories always came back, sharp and unyielding.

Three years ago, I'd been an MI6 agent on a mission in Paris. The objective was clear: infiltrate an underground network dealing in stolen art and take down the key players.

But Victor Williams had outplayed us all. The intel was bogus, the operation compromised, and I'd barely made it out alive. The mission's failure cost me more than my career—it left me with a searing need for revenge and a deep distrust of everyone around me.

And then there was Chloe.

I hadn't thought about her in a long time. At least, that's what I told myself. Chloe Laurent was the enigma in Victor's twisted game. I first saw her at one of his art galas, standing amidst the crowd with an air of quiet sophistication.

She was Victor's lover and business partner, yet something about her felt out of place. When everything went to hell, she was the one who took the fall, framed by Victor without a second thought. I'd watched her life implode from the shadows, unable to intervene.

The ice in my glass melted, diluting the whiskey. I took a sip, savouring the burn as it slid down my throat. Since leaving MI6 special force, I'd become a private investigator, dealing in cases that operated in the grey areas of the law.

My contacts were a motley crew—ex-spies, mercenaries, and underworld operatives. It was a life lived in the shadows, but it suited me. Or so I'd convinced myself.

My phone buzzed on the bar, breaking my reverie. I glanced at the screen, and my pulse quickened. The message was brief but charged with significance.

We need to talk. - Chloe

For a moment, I just stared at it. Chloe. I hadn't heard from her since her trial. She'd vanished after her release, leaving a cloud of rumours in her wake. I'd tried to keep tabs on her, but she'd become a ghost, slipping through the cracks of the world I knew so well.

I quickly typed a response, arranging a meeting at a quiet café in Montmartre. I finished my drink and left the bar, the cool night air hitting my face. As I walked down the narrow streets, anticipation bubbled within me—a mix of dread and excitement. Chloe reaching out could only mean one thing: she was ready to fight back.

The café was a small, unassuming place, tucked away from the main streets. I arrived early, scanning the room for any potential threats. Satisfied, I took a seat by the window, my back to the wall. The place was quiet, perfect for a discreet meeting.

When Chloe walked in, my breath caught. She looked different—her long hair was now cut into a stylish bob, and she wore dark, simple clothes that made her blend into the shadows.

But her eyes... her eyes were the same, sharp and determined. She spotted me and walked over; her steps confident but cautious.

We sat in silence for a moment, the tension between us palpable. Then, she spoke, her voice steady but tinged with an undercurrent of tension.

"Mr. Bennet," she began, meeting my gaze. "I need your help."

I leaned back, scrutinizing her. "What happened to staying out of the game?" I asked, unable to keep the sarcasm out of my voice. "You disappeared, Chloe. I thought you were done."

She sighed, her expression softening. "I tried," she admitted. "But I can't let him get away with it. Victor ruined my life. He took everything from me, and he's still out there, living his perfect little life. I can't just walk away."

I nodded, understanding all too well the need for closure. "So, what's the plan?" I asked, leaning forward. "You wouldn't have come to me if you didn't have one."

Chloe pulled a small notebook from her bag and slid it across the table. I opened it and quickly scanned the contents—blueprints of Victor's new gallery, names of his associates, and a list of his illegal activities. She'd been busy.

"I want to take him down," she said, her voice firm. "Not just for revenge, but to expose him for what he really is. He's involved in more than just art theft, Adrian. There's human trafficking, money laundering... I want to destroy his empire, piece by piece."

I closed the notebook and looked up at her. The fire in her eyes was unmistakable. It was both admirable and concerning. Taking down Victor wouldn't be easy; it would be dangerous. But then again, danger was something I was familiar with.

A slow grin spread across my face. "Count me in," I said. "But we need to do this right. No room for mistakes."

She nodded, a small smile touching her lips. "Agreed. Let's make sure Victor regrets the day he crossed us."

As we sat there, hashing out the details of our plan, a sense of purpose filled me. This wasn't just another mission; it was a chance for redemption. For both of us. And as I looked at Chloe, I knew that whatever happened, we would face it together.

The game was on, and I was ready to play.

2

Chloe

The early evening sun cast long shadows across the cobblestone streets of Montmartre as I made my way to the small café where I'd agreed to meet Adrian. My heart pounded with a mix of nervousness and anticipation. It had been three years since I'd last seen him, three years filled with darkness, isolation, and the slow, painful process of rebuilding my life. And now, as I approached the café, the weight of those years felt heavier than ever.

I paused outside the door, taking a deep breath. I was here for a reason—to finally bring Victor down and reclaim my life. Yet, the thought of seeing Adrian again stirred something inside me that I couldn't quite suppress. We'd been on opposite sides of a chaotic, dangerous world, yet there was a connection between us, a shared understanding that went beyond words. I had tried to keep my feelings buried, but they had a way of resurfacing, especially now.

Pushing the door open, I stepped into the café, my eyes scanning the room. There he was, sitting by the window, looking just as I remembered—rugged, intense, with those piercing blue eyes that seemed to see everything. As our eyes met, a jolt of electricity shot through me. For a moment, I felt like the world had narrowed to just the two of us. I quickly composed myself and walked over, my steps steady, even if my heart was racing.

We exchanged brief pleasantries, but the air between us was thick with unspoken words. Adrian's gaze was as inscrutable as ever, but there was a softness in his eyes that hadn't been there before. I tried to keep my emotions in check, focusing on the task at hand. We were here for a purpose, and I couldn't afford to let old feelings cloud my judgment.

As we discussed the plan, I couldn't help but steal glances at him. His presence was reassuring, a reminder of the strength and resourcefulness that had always drawn me to him. Yet, it was also a painful reminder of what could never be.

Our worlds had been too different, our paths too divergent. I knew that rekindling any kind of relationship, even a professional one, would be complicated. But as we hashed out the details of our operation, I realized just how much I needed him, not just as an ally, but as a confidant, someone who understood the darkness I had faced.

The night of the gala arrived faster than I expected. As I stood in front of the mirror, adjusting my dress, I felt a wave of anxiety wash over me. This would be my first public appearance since my fall from grace.

The thought of facing the judgmental eyes of high society, the whispers, and the veiled insults filled me with dread. But I had no choice. If we were going to expose Victor, we needed to play the game.

I slipped into a sleek black gown, simple yet elegant, paired with a diamond necklace that had once belonged to my mother. It was a small piece of my past that I held onto, a reminder of who I used to be. I took one last look in the mirror, straightened my shoulders, and left the room.

At the gala, the opulence was overwhelming. Chandeliers sparkled above, casting a golden glow over the crowd of well-dressed elites. The room buzzed with laughter and conversation, a stark contrast to the turmoil churning inside me. I felt out of place, like an imposter among these people who had once been my peers.

Adrian was already there, blending effortlessly into the crowd. He looked sharp in a tailored suit, his eyes scanning the room with a practiced vigilance. Our eyes met briefly, and he gave me a subtle nod. It was a small gesture, but it grounded me, reminding me of why we were here.

As the evening progressed, we slipped into our roles with practiced ease. Adrian was the charming guest, engaging in light conversation and keeping an eye on Victor's associates. I played the part of the disgraced but resilient art dealer, making polite small talk with old acquaintances who pretended to be surprised by my presence. The whispers and sideways glances were inevitable, but I held my head high, refusing to let their judgment faze me.

Despite the outward calm, I felt like I was walking a tightrope, balancing my emotions and the mission. Being so close to Adrian, I couldn't ignore the unresolved feelings that lingered between us.

Every glance, every word exchanged carried an unspoken tension, a reminder of the connection we shared. I tried to keep my focus, reminding myself that this was a professional relationship, nothing more. But in the dim lights and soft music, it was hard to ignore the past, the what-ifs that had haunted me for years.

At one point, we found ourselves alone on the balcony, away from the prying eyes and the suffocating atmosphere inside. The cool night air was a welcome relief, and I took a deep breath, trying to steady my nerves. Adrian stood beside me, his presence a comforting anchor. For a moment, we stood in silence, the weight of our shared history hanging between us.

"How are you holding up?" he asked, his voice low and sincere.

I glanced at him, offering a small, tight-lipped smile. "As well as can be expected," I replied. "It's strange, being back in this world."

He nodded; his expression thoughtful. "You're doing great," he said, a hint of admiration in his tone. "You've always been strong, Chloe."

His words caught me off guard, a warmth spreading through me despite my best efforts to stay composed. I looked away, staring out at the city lights, feeling the familiar ache of longing and regret. I knew I couldn't let these emotions distract me, but standing there with Adrian, it was hard to separate the past from the present.

Before I could respond, the moment was interrupted by the sound of footsteps. We turned to see one of Victor's associates approaching, a predatory smile on his lips.

The man's eyes flicked between us, a glint of recognition in his gaze. The air grew tense, and I forced a polite smile, slipping back into my role.

Adrian stepped forward, smoothly diverting the conversation and drawing the man's attention away from me. I watched him work, admiring his effortless charm and quick thinking.

It was a reminder of why I had reached out to him in the first place. He was my ally, my partner in this dangerous game. Whatever unresolved feelings existed between us; they had to take a back seat to the mission.

As the night wore on, we continued to play our parts, gathering information and subtly undermining Victor's carefully crafted image. Despite the challenges, I felt a renewed sense of purpose, a determination to see this through. And with Adrian by my side, I knew we had a chance.

Leaving the gala, I couldn't shake the mixture of emotions swirling inside me. The evening had been a success, but it had also reopened old wounds. I glanced at Adrian as we walked out into the night, his face unreadable.

There was so much left unsaid between us, so many questions that lingered in the air.

But as we headed back into the shadows, ready to continue our fight, I knew one thing for certain: I wasn't alone in this. And maybe, just maybe, that would make all the difference.

3

Adrian

The night air was crisp as we approached the back entrance of Victor's gallery. The moon hung high in the sky, casting a pale glow over the city. The streets were quiet, save for the occasional sound of a car passing by or a distant conversation. It was the perfect cover for what we were about to do.

As we stood in the shadows, my mind was focused, my senses heightened. Every detail of the plan played out in my head like a well-rehearsed dance. We had one shot to get this right, and failure wasn't an option.

I glanced at Chloe beside me, her face set with determination. Even in the dim light, she looked composed, her eyes sharp and alert. There was something about seeing her like this, ready for the danger ahead, that filled me with a mix of pride and protectiveness.

It was strange, feeling this way. As a former MI6 agent, I'd worked with plenty of capable people, but Chloe was different. She wasn't trained for this life; she hadn't chosen it. Yet here she was, standing tall, ready to face whatever came our way. It was hard not to admire her courage, even if it complicated things. I couldn't afford to be distracted by my feelings, not now.

I signalled to Chloe, and we moved in sync, slipping through the alley toward the door. The lock was simple, easily bypassed with a few deft moves of my tools. As the door clicked open, we exchanged a quick nod, then stepped inside. The gallery was dark, the only light coming from the emergency exit signs. We moved silently, navigating the familiar space with ease.

Our target was Victor's office, a room tucked away at the back of the building. According to our intel, it was where he kept the documents that would expose his illegal activities. It was also heavily guarded, with alarms and security cameras. But we had planned for that. Chloe had managed to get a job as a temporary curator, giving her access to the gallery's security system. She'd spent weeks studying the layout, memorizing the guards' schedules, and finding the weaknesses in the system.

We reached the hallway leading to the office. I crouched down, pulling out a small device from my bag. It was a signal jammer, designed to disable the cameras and alarms temporarily. I handed it to Chloe, trusting her to do the honours. As she activated it, I couldn't help but watch her, admiring the way she handled herself. She was cool, collected, every movement precise and deliberate. It was clear she'd been preparing for this moment, and I couldn't deny the admiration I felt for her.

With the cameras and alarms disabled, we made our way to the office door. I picked the lock quickly, and we slipped inside. The room was just as we'd expected—sleek, modern, with an air of understated luxury. Victor had always had a taste for the finer things. I moved to the desk, searching for the hidden safe. Chloe stood by the door, keeping watch, her eyes scanning the hallway.

The safe was concealed behind a painting, just as we'd suspected. I pulled it aside, revealing the keypad. As I worked on cracking the code, I felt Chloe's presence beside me, her eyes on the door. It was comforting, knowing she had my back. But it was also distracting. I could feel the tension between us, the unspoken words that hung in the air.

The safe clicked open, and I pulled out the documents. There they were—proof of Victor's involvement in human trafficking, money laundering, and a dozen other crimes. It was enough to bring him down, to destroy everything he'd built. I handed the files to Chloe, our fingers brushing for a brief moment. It was a small touch, but it sent a jolt through me. I quickly pulled away, focusing on the task at hand.

As Chloe scanned the documents, I couldn't help but notice the way her face lit up with determination. She was in her element, and it was impossible not to be drawn to her. But I knew better than to let my guard down. There was too much at stake, and I couldn't afford to let my feelings cloud my judgment.

"Let's get out of here," I whispered, nodding toward the door.

We slipped out of the office, making our way back through the gallery. My mind was racing, not just with the success of the mission, but with the conflicting emotions swirling inside me. Chloe had always been a mystery to me, a puzzle I couldn't quite solve. And now, standing beside her in the dark, I felt a pull I couldn't ignore.

As we exited the building and made our way to the car, I kept my eyes on the street, alert for any signs of trouble. The night was quiet, the city asleep. It seemed we'd pulled it off without a hitch. But the real challenge was just beginning. We had the evidence, but now we had to use it to bring Victor down. And in the midst of it all, I had to keep my emotions in check.

Once we were safely inside the car, I let out a breath I hadn't realized I'd been holding. Chloe sat beside me; her eyes focused on the road ahead. There was a moment of silence, a calm after the storm. Then, she turned to me, her expression serious.

"We did it," she said, her voice steady but filled with an underlying intensity.

I nodded, meeting her gaze. "Yeah," I replied, my voice low. "We did."

As we drove away, the weight of what we'd accomplished settled over me. We'd taken the first step in bringing Victor to justice, but there was still a long road ahead. And as much as I tried to deny it, my feelings for Chloe were becoming harder to ignore. The heist had been a success, but the real battle was just beginning.

As the city lights blurred past, I glanced at
Chloe, a mix of emotions churning inside me.
Pride, admiration, and something deeper,
something more complicated. I knew I had to
keep my distance, to stay focused on the mission.
But as the night wore on, I couldn't shake the
feeling that this was just the beginning of
something much bigger—something that could
change everything.

4

Chloe

The adrenaline had barely begun to fade when we found ourselves in the thick of it again. It seemed like no matter where we turned, danger followed. I couldn't shake the feeling that we were being hunted, each close call a reminder that Victor was always one step ahead. It was a sickening game of cat and mouse, and we were the prey.

We moved from safe house to safe house, never staying in one place for too long. My nerves were constantly on edge, every creak of a floorboard or rustle of leaves outside a potential threat. Adrian remained calm; his years of experience evident in the way he navigated each new situation. But even he couldn't hide the strain. The lines around his eyes deepened, and there were moments when his guard slipped, revealing a weariness that mirrored my own.

One night, after narrowly escaping a trap laid by Victor's men, we found ourselves in a small, nondescript motel on the outskirts of Paris. The room was sparse, the dim light casting long shadows on the walls. I sat on the edge of the bed, my hands still shaking from the close call. Adrian was across the room, checking the locks on the door and windows, making sure we were secure.

I watched him, a mix of emotions swirling inside me. He'd saved my life more times than I could count, but it wasn't just that. Over the past few weeks, I'd come to rely on him, not just as a partner, but as a confidant. There was a comfort in his presence, a sense of safety that I hadn't felt in years. But with that comfort came confusion. My feelings for him were growing stronger, and it terrified me. I couldn't afford to get distracted, not when we were so close to bringing Victor down. But every time I looked at Adrian, I felt a pull I couldn't ignore.

As he finished his checks, he glanced over at me, his eyes meeting mine. There was a moment of silence, a charged tension between us. I looked away, trying to gather my thoughts. I couldn't let my emotions get the better of me, not now.

"We're safe for now," he said, his voice low and steady. "But we need to be careful. Victor's not going to give up easily."

I nodded, swallowing hard. "I know," I replied, my voice barely above a whisper. "I just... I can't help but feel like we're missing something. He's always one step ahead, always knows where to find us."

Adrian walked over and sat beside me, the bed dipping slightly under his weight. "Victor's a smart man," he said, his tone thoughtful. "He has resources, contacts. But so do we. We'll find a way to outsmart him."

There was a confidence in his voice that was reassuring, but also unsettling. I'd been so focused on my own vendetta that I hadn't stopped to question Adrian's motivations. He'd been with me every step of the way, but I realized I didn't know why. Was it just about taking down a mutual enemy, or was there something more?

"Why are you doing this, Adrian?" I blurted out, the question escaping before I could stop it. "You left that life behind. You didn't have to come back."

He looked at me, a flicker of something unreadable in his eyes. For a moment, I thought he might evade the question, but then he sighed, running a hand through his hair.

"I owe you," he said finally, his voice tinged with a hint of regret. "For what happened three years ago. For not stopping Victor when I had the chance. This is my way of making things right."

I studied his face, trying to gauge the sincerity in his words. There was something more, something he wasn't telling me. But I couldn't press him, not when we were both so vulnerable. I had to trust him, at least for now.

As the night wore on, we talked about the next steps, our voices low and cautious. Every plan we made, every move we considered was laced with the underlying threat of danger. But amidst the chaos, there was a strange sense of camaraderie, a bond that had formed between us. I found myself opening up to Adrian in ways I hadn't expected, sharing my fears, my doubts, and the weight of the past that still haunted me.

Yet, as much as I trusted him, there was a part of me that couldn't shake the suspicion that he was holding something back. It was in the way he spoke, the careful choice of words, the occasional hesitations. There was a depth to his involvement that went beyond just righting a wrong. But every time I tried to probe deeper, he'd deflect, steering the conversation back to the task at hand.

As the first light of dawn filtered through the thin curtains, we finally settled into an uneasy silence. Adrian stretched out on the small couch, his eyes closing as exhaustion took over.

I lay on the bed, staring up at the ceiling, my mind racing. The line between ally and something more had blurred, and I wasn't sure where we stood.

I turned my head to look at him, taking in the sharp lines of his face, the stubble on his jaw, the way his chest rose and fell with each breath. There was so much left unsaid between us, so many questions that lingered in the air. But for now, I had to focus on the mission. We were running out of time, and the noose around Victor's neck was tightening.

As sleep finally claimed me, one thought echoed in my mind: I couldn't let my feelings for Adrian distract me, but I couldn't deny them either. We were in this together, for better or worse. And as much as I tried to fight it, I knew that my heart was already entangled in this dangerous game. The cat and mouse chase with Victor was far from over, but so was the struggle within myself.

Aditi. J

5

Adrian

The safe house was a nondescript building on the outskirts of the city, its plain facade blending seamlessly into the quiet suburban neighbourhood. It was one of the few places we could truly let our guard down, a rare sanctuary amidst the chaos. As we entered, the weight of the past few weeks seemed to settle heavily on my shoulders. Every narrow escape, every moment spent looking over our shoulders had taken its toll. And yet, the real challenge was only just beginning.

I locked the door behind us, securing the multiple deadbolts and setting the alarm. The silence was thick, the kind that followed a storm. Chloe moved quietly, setting her bag down on the worn couch, her expression unreadable.

I watched her for a moment, taking in the lines of tension in her posture, the way her eyes flickered with an emotion she was trying to hide. She had been through so much, and yet here she was, still standing, still fighting.

I took a deep breath, trying to steady the tumult of emotions inside me. There were things I needed to say, truths that had been gnawing at me for years.

But as much as I wanted to open up, to tell her everything, a part of me was afraid. Afraid of how she would react, of what it would mean for us. But I knew I couldn't hold back any longer. She deserved to know the truth, even if it changed everything.

"Chloe," I began, my voice quiet but firm. She looked up at me, her eyes searching mine. There was a flicker of something in her gaze... curiosity, maybe, or apprehension.

I swallowed hard, trying to find the right words. "There's something I need to tell you. About the past, about... us."

She sat down, her posture guarded. I joined her on the couch, the distance between us feeling like a chasm. For a moment, we just sat there, the room filled with an uneasy silence. I could feel my heart pounding in my chest, a mixture of fear and anticipation.

I had spent years running from my feelings, burying them under layers of regret and guilt. But now, in this quiet, secluded space, there was no more hiding.

"I know I've always been a mystery to you," I said finally, my voice rough with emotion. "I know I've kept you in the dark about a lot of things. But the truth is, I've always cared about you, Chloe. More than I ever let on."

She didn't say anything, but her eyes softened, a glimmer of vulnerability peeking through. It was enough to give me the courage to continue.

"I left MI6 because I couldn't stand the person I'd become," I confessed, the words spilling out like a long-held secret. "I did things, made choices that I'm not proud of. And when everything fell apart with Victor, I saw it as my chance to walk away, to start over. But... I never stopped thinking about you. From the first time I saw you, when you were with victor. I never stopped caring."

Her expression remained unreadable, but there was a tension in her posture that told me she was listening, really listening. I took a deep breath, pushing forward.

"I know I've made mistakes," I continued, my voice faltering. "And I know that being with me complicates things. But I can't deny how I feel anymore. Not when we're constantly facing danger, not when I could lose you at any moment."

There was a long pause, the air between us charged with unspoken emotions. Chloe looked away, her fingers twisting in her lap. When she finally spoke, her voice was barely above a whisper.

"I've always wondered," she said, her tone tinged with sadness. "Why you never reached out. Why you never tried to stop Victor when you had the chance."

Her words hit me like a punch to the gut. She had every right to be angry, to question my actions. I had walked away, leaving her to face the consequences alone. I had my reasons, but they felt hollow in the face of her pain.

"I'm sorry," I said, the words heavy with sincerity. "I thought I was doing the right thing, but I was wrong. I should have been there for you. I should have fought harder."

She turned to me, her eyes glistening with unshed tears. "It's not just about Victor," she murmured. "It's about everything. The lies, the secrets... the way we both ran away from what we felt."

I reached out, gently taking her hand in mine. The touch was electric, a connection that had always been there, simmering beneath the surface. "I know," I whispered, my voice thick with emotion. "But I'm here now. And I won't run away again."

The silence that followed was filled with a thousand unspoken words. Chloe's hand tightened around mine, and for a moment, it felt like the world had stopped spinning. It was just the two of us, facing the truth of our pasts and the uncertain future that lay ahead.

Before I could say anything else, Chloe leaned in, her lips meeting mine in a soft, tentative kiss. It was a kiss filled with longing, with the weight of years of unspoken emotions. I felt my heart race, a rush of heat flooding through me. I deepened the kiss, pulling her closer, feeling the warmth of her body against mine.

It was as if the floodgates had opened, the dam of restraint and caution breaking under the force of our desire. The kiss grew more urgent, more desperate, a release of all the emotions we'd been holding back. I felt her hands in my hair, pulling me closer, and I responded in kind, my fingers tracing the curve of her back.

We pulled away, breathless, our foreheads resting against each other. For a moment, we just sat there, the room filled with the sound of our ragged breathing. There was a vulnerability in Chloe's eyes, a rawness that mirrored my own.

"I've wanted this for so long," she confessed, her voice barely above a whisper. "But I was afraid. Afraid of getting hurt again, afraid of what it would mean."

I cupped her face in my hands, my thumbs gently brushing away the tears that had escaped. "I'm here," I repeated, my voice steady. "And I'm not going anywhere. Whatever happens, we'll face it together."

She nodded, a small, tremulous smile breaking through the tears. We stayed like that for a while, holding each other, finding comfort in the shared warmth of our bodies. It was a moment of peace amidst the storm, a brief respite from the danger that loomed over us.

As the night wore on, we lay together, wrapped in each other's arms. The tension and fear that had plagued us seemed to melt away, replaced by a sense of calm.

 I felt a renewed determination, a resolve to protect Chloe at all costs. I knew the road ahead would be dangerous, filled with uncertainty and threats. But for the first time in a long time, I felt hope.

Hope that we could find a way out of this mess, hope that we could build something new together. And as I held Chloe close, listening to the steady rhythm of her breathing, I knew that I would do whatever it took to keep her safe.

Even if it meant facing the demons of my past, even if it meant risking everything.

Because in that quiet, stolen moment, I realized something that had been growing inside me for years: I loved her.

And I wasn't going to let anything stand in the way of that. Not Victor, not the dangers we faced, not even my own fears.

As the first light of dawn began to filter through the windows, I closed my eyes, holding Chloe close. We had a long road ahead of us, but for now, we had each other. And that was enough.

6

Chloe

The air in the room was thick with tension, the kind that made it hard to breathe. My mind was reeling, trying to process the scene that had just unfolded. Isabelle, one of the few people I thought I could trust, had betrayed us. It felt like the ground had been ripped out from under me, leaving me floundering in a sea of confusion and anger.

The sting of betrayal burned deep. Isabelle had been more than just a contact; she'd been a friend, someone I'd confided in during those long, lonely nights when the weight of my mission felt too heavy to bear. But now, as I replayed the look on her face—the cold, calculating expression as she handed over our location to Victor's men—I felt a cold fury simmering beneath the surface.

Adrian and I had narrowly escaped, but the damage was done. Isabelle had sold us out, and for what? Money? Power? The questions gnawed

at me, each one a sharp reminder of the precariousness of our situation. The safe house that had been our sanctuary was now compromised, and we were back to square one, running for our lives.

As we made our way to a new hideout—an apartment on the outskirts of the city—I couldn't shake the feeling of unease. Adrian was silent beside me, his jaw clenched, eyes forward. He hadn't said much since the betrayal, and I wondered what was going through his mind.

Was he as blindsided as I was? Or had he known all along and chosen not to tell me?

The thought was a bitter one. Despite everything we'd shared, the intimate moments and whispered confessions, there was still a part of Adrian that remained a mystery. And now, with Isabelle's treachery looming over us, I couldn't help but question everything. Though Isabelle was a person from his past, did Adrian's feelings for her still cloud his judgment? Was he still harbouring some lingering attachment to her?

The car came to a stop, and Adrian cut the engine. We sat in the quiet, the only sound the

distant hum of the city. I looked at him, searching for answers in his expression. His face was hard, a mask of unreadable emotions. It was like a wall had gone up between us, and I didn't know how to break through.

"How long?" I asked, my voice barely above a whisper. The question hung in the air, heavy with implications. I needed to know how long Isabelle had been working against us, how long Adrian had known.

He turned to me, his eyes dark and troubled. "I didn't know," he said, his voice rough. "Not until today."

I wanted to believe him, but the doubt gnawed at me. Isabelle had been his contact; someone he'd vouched for. If she was compromised, how could I trust that Adrian wasn't, too? The paranoia was insidious, working its way into my thoughts. But as much as I wanted to accuse him, to lay the blame at his feet, I couldn't. Not without more evidence, not without unravelling the tangled web we found ourselves in.

I took a deep breath, trying to steady the swirl of emotions inside me. "She was your contact," I said, my voice steady despite the turmoil I felt. "How could you not know?"

Adrian's expression tightened, a flicker of pain crossing his features. "She was more than just a contact," he admitted, the words like a confession. "She was someone I... cared about. But that was a long time ago, Chloe. Things change. People change."

There it was, the admission I'd been dreading. A part of me had suspected, but hearing it out loud was like a punch to the gut. Isabelle wasn't just some informant; she'd been a part of Adrian's life, a part he hadn't shared with me. And now, that part had come back to haunt us, to tear apart the fragile trust we'd built.

"Do you still have feelings for her?" The question slipped out before I could stop it, raw and unfiltered. It was the heart of my fear, the nagging doubt that had been festering since Isabelle's betrayal.

Adrian looked away, his jaw clenching. The silence stretched, each second a knife twisting in my chest. Finally, he spoke, his voice low and controlled. "No," he said, meeting my gaze with a fierce intensity. "Whatever we had, it's in the past. My only concern now is keeping you safe."

I wanted to believe him, wanted to take solace in his words. But the uncertainty lingered, a shadow over our relationship. Trust was a fragile thing, and Isabelle's betrayal had shattered it. I felt the sting of it keenly, the sense of isolation creeping in. Even with Adrian by my side, I felt alone, adrift in a sea of danger and deception.

As we made our way into the apartment, the reality of our situation settled over me like a heavy cloak. Victor's network was vast, his reach extending further than we'd anticipated.

Isabelle's betrayal was proof of that, a stark reminder of the danger we were in. We couldn't trust anyone, not even the people we thought were allies.

The apartment was sparse, a bare-bones safe house with minimal furnishings. I dropped my bag on the floor, the weight of the day crashing over me. Adrian moved around the room,

checking the windows and doors, his movements precise and efficient. I watched him, the tension between us palpable.

"We need to figure out our next move," he said, his tone all business. "Victor's not going to stop, and now that Isabelle's turned, we have to be even more careful."

I nodded, but my mind was elsewhere. I couldn't stop thinking about the betrayal, the feeling of being blindsided by someone I trusted. It was a harsh reminder of the stakes we were playing for, and the lengths Victor would go to protect his empire. But more than that, it was a reminder of the fragility of trust, and how easily it could be broken.

As I sat on the edge of the bed, I felt a cold determination settle over me. I couldn't afford to be naive, couldn't afford to let my emotions cloud my judgment. Isabelle's betrayal had hurt, but it had also steeled my resolve. I would not back down, not now, not ever. I would see this through, no matter the cost.

Adrian sat down beside me, his expression softening. He reached out, taking my hand in his. The gesture was small, but it was enough to break through the wall I'd built around myself. I looked at him, seeing the concern and regret in his eyes. For a moment, the tension between us eased, replaced by a shared understanding of the gravity of our situation.

"I'm sorry," he said quietly, his thumb brushing over my knuckles. "For everything. For not seeing this coming, for putting you in danger. But we're in this together, and I won't let anything happen to you."

I felt a lump in my throat, the sincerity in his voice cutting through my doubts. I squeezed his hand, a silent acknowledgment of the trust I was choosing to place in him, despite everything. We were in this together, for better or worse. And as much as the betrayal stung, as much as the uncertainty gnawed at me, I knew we had to keep moving forward.

As the night wore on, we sat together, planning our next steps. The weight of our mission pressed down on us, but there was also a flicker of hope. We had come this far, survived this long, and we weren't going to stop now.

Victor's network was vast, but so was our determination. We would find a way to bring him down, to dismantle his empire piece by piece.

47

And as I looked at Adrian, his face etched with resolve, I felt a surge of defiance. Isabelle's betrayal had shaken me, but it hadn't broken me. I would not let Victor win. I would not let fear control me. We would see this through, together.

No matter what it took.

7

Adrian

The room was dimly lit, the only source of light coming from the computer screen in front of me. The safe house was quiet, the air thick with tension and the weight of our discoveries. I leaned back in my chair, rubbing my eyes, the glow of the screen burning into my retinas. The information I'd unearthed was worse than I had anticipated—far worse.

Victor's crimes had always been shrouded in mystery, whispered about in the darkest corners of the underworld. But now, as the details of his human trafficking ring came into focus, I felt a cold dread settle in my chest.

The scale of it was monstrous, an intricate network spanning multiple countries, exploiting vulnerable men, women, and children. The realization hit me like a punch to the gut, the full horror of it sinking in.

I stared at the list of names on the screen, a catalogue of lives stolen and sold, each one a reminder of the depth of Victor's depravity. It was a reminder that this mission wasn't just about revenge or redemption.

It was about justice for those who couldn't fight for themselves, about stopping a monster who preyed on the innocent. The weight of it all pressed down on me, a suffocating burden I couldn't escape.

Chloe was asleep in the next room, exhausted from the day's events. Her face had been paled; her eyes haunted by the betrayal we'd uncovered.

Isabelle's treachery had cut deep, not just because of the danger it put us in, but because it had shattered the fragile trust Chloe and I were trying to rebuild. But as much as I wanted to focus on that, to sort through the tangled mess of our emotions, there were more pressing matters at hand.

I turned back to the screen, my fingers flying over the keyboard as I pieced together the fragments of Victor's operation. He had always been meticulous, leaving little to chance. But even the most careful criminals made mistakes, and I was determined to find them.

The evidence we'd gathered so far painted a grim picture: shell companies, offshore accounts, and a web of contacts in law enforcement and government. It was a sickeningly efficient machine, designed to exploit and discard human lives for profit.

As I delved deeper, a pattern began to emerge. Victor's reach extended far beyond the trafficking ring; he had his hands in illegal arms dealing, drug smuggling, and political corruption. It was an empire built on the suffering of others, a testament to his ruthless ambition.

The more I uncovered, the more I realized the enormity of what we were up against. This wasn't just a mission for revenge; it was a battle against a man who thought himself untouchable.

I leaned back in my chair, a bitter taste in my mouth. The realization was sobering. For so long, my focus had been on getting back at Victor, on avenging the wrongs he'd done to me and Chloe.

But now, as the full scope of his crimes came to light, I felt a shift in my perspective. This wasn't just about us anymore. It was about all the people Victor had hurt, the lives he had

destroyed. And I couldn't, in good conscience, walk away from that.

A knock on the door startled me out of my thoughts. I glanced at the clock—it was late, far too late for visitors. I moved quietly, reaching for the gun I'd placed on the table.

My heart pounded in my chest, a mix of adrenaline and fear coursing through me. I approached the door cautiously, peering through the peephole. To my relief, it was Chloe.

I opened the door, and she slipped inside, her expression tense. "Couldn't sleep," she murmured, her voice barely above a whisper. She glanced at the computer screen, her brow furrowing as she took in the information displayed. "Find anything?"

I nodded, gesturing for her to sit down. "More than I wanted to," I admitted, the heaviness in my voice evident. I pulled up a map, highlighting the various locations tied to Victor's operation. "He's got his fingers in everything. Trafficking, drugs, weapons... It's worse than we thought."

Chloe's face paled as she absorbed the details, her eyes darkening with anger and disgust. "All those people..." she whispered, her voice breaking. "We have to stop him, Adrian. We can't let him get away with this."

Her words resonated with me, a call to action that I couldn't ignore. I reached out, taking her hand in mine. It was a simple gesture, but it grounded me, reminded me of why we were doing this. Chloe's determination mirrored my own, a fierce resolve to bring Victor to justice.

"I know," I said, my voice steady. "But we have to be smart about this. Victor's not going to go down easily. We need to find a way to expose him, to take down his entire operation. And we need to do it without getting ourselves killed."

Chloe nodded, a determined look in her eyes. "We can do this," she said, her voice firm. "We have to. For all the people he's hurt."

Her words were a reminder of the stakes, of the lives hanging in the balance. As I looked into her eyes, I felt a renewed sense of purpose.

This wasn't just about settling old scores or righting personal wrongs. It was about something bigger, something more important. It was about standing up to a monster and fighting for those who couldn't fight for themselves.

Gently squeezing her hand in mine, I traced circles on her fingers with my thumb and then I pulled her onto my lap.

As we sat together, mapping out our next moves, I felt a strange sense of calm wash over me. The road ahead was dangerous, filled with uncertainty and risk.

But we were in this together, united by a common goal. And as long as we had each other, I knew we could face whatever came our way.

For the first time in a long time, I felt a glimmer of hope. Hope that we could make a difference,

that we could bring Victor's empire crashing down. It was a dangerous mission, but it was worth the risk. Because in the end, it wasn't just about revenge or redemption. It was about justice.

55

And we would stop at nothing to see it done.

8

Chloe

The night air was thick with tension, a palpable electricity that prickled at my skin. As we approached the compound, my heart pounded in my chest, a steady drumbeat that matched the thrum of adrenaline coursing through my veins. The plan was simple—get in, get the hostages, and get out. But nothing about this mission felt simple. Every step forward felt like a step deeper into the lion's den.

I glanced at Adrian, his face a mask of focus and determination. His presence was a steadying force, a reminder that I wasn't alone in this fight. We were in this together, for better or worse. It was a strange comfort, knowing that no matter what happened, he would be by my side.

The compound loomed ahead, a dark silhouette against the night sky. My fingers tightened around the handle of my gun, the cold metal a reassuring weight in my hand.

We'd prepared for this moment, gone over the plan a dozen times. But no amount of preparation could quell the fear gnawing at my gut. This was it—the culmination of everything we'd been working toward.

As we reached the outer fence, I crouched low, signalling to the others. The team moved silently, their movements fluid and precise. We'd managed to gather a small group of allies of Adrian, they also wanted to see criminal like victor to be brought down. They were a motley crew, but they were determined, and that was what mattered.

Adrian handed me a pair of wire cutters, and I set to work, slicing through the fence with practiced ease. The metal gave way, and we slipped through the gap, moving swiftly across the compound grounds.

 My eyes scanned the area, searching for any signs of movement. The guards were on high alert, but we'd timed our approach perfectly, slipping in during a shift change. We had a narrow window, and we had to make it count.

The building where the hostages were being held was a squat, nondescript structure at the back of the compound. It looked unassuming, but I knew better.

Inside, there were people—innocent lives that Victor had stolen and trapped in his web of exploitation. The thought of it filled me with a cold fury, a burning desire to see him pay for his crimes.

We reached the building, and I signalled for the team to take their positions. Adrian and I would lead the charge, with the others providing backup. It was a risky plan, but it was our best shot. I took a deep breath, steadying myself. This was it—the moment of truth.

With a nod from Adrian, I kicked open the door, the sound echoing through the hallway. The guards inside reacted quickly, raising their weapons, but we were faster.

Adrian took down the first two with a series of precise shots, and I followed suit, my training kicking in as I moved through the space. It was chaotic, the air filled with the sound of gunfire

and shouts. But I stayed focused, my mind laser-sharp as I cleared room after room.

As we fought our way through the building, I couldn't help but reflect on how far I'd come. A year ago, I was a journalist, chasing stories and exposing corruption from the safety of my desk.

Now, I was here, in the thick of it, risking my life to save others. The transformation was staggering, and it was all because of Victor— because of the way he'd torn my life apart and set me on this path.

But as much as I hated him, as much as I wanted to see him suffer, I couldn't ignore the toll this quest for vengeance had taken on me. The sleepless nights, the constant fear and paranoia—it had changed me, hardened me in ways I never expected. I wasn't the same person I was before, and I wasn't sure if that was a good thing.

We reached the main room, where the hostages were being held. The sight was gut-wrenching—men and women, bound and gagged, their faces pale and hollow. It was a stark reminder of the stakes, of the lives Victor had destroyed.

My heart ached for them, but there was no time for sympathy. We had to move quickly.

Adrian covered me as I rushed to the hostages, cutting their restraints and helping them to their feet. Their eyes were wide with fear and confusion, but there was a glimmer of hope in their expressions—a spark that gave me strength. "You're safe now," I murmured, my voice firm. "We're getting you out of here."

As the team led the hostages out of the building, I stayed behind with Adrian, making sure the path was clear. The adrenaline was still pumping, but beneath it, there was a gnawing uncertainty.

This was only the beginning. Victor was still out there, and he wouldn't take this lightly. We had struck a blow, but the war was far from over.

We reached the rendezvous point, the night air cool against my skin. The hostages were safe, the team accounted for. It should have been a victory, a moment of triumph.

But as I looked at the faces of the people we'd saved, I felt a pang of doubt. Was this enough? Would it ever be enough?

Adrian's hand on my shoulder pulled me from my thoughts. His eyes met mine, a silent understanding passing between us. He saw the turmoil in my expression, the questions I couldn't voice. And in that moment, I knew I wasn't alone in my uncertainty. He felt it too—the weight of our choices, the cost of our mission.

As we made our way back to the safe house, I felt a strange mix of emotions. Relief, for the lives we'd saved. Pride, for the strength we'd shown. But also fear, for the battles still to come. I glanced at Adrian; his profile sharp against the night. He was my anchor, my partner in this chaotic mess. And as long as we had each other, I knew we could face whatever came our way.

The road ahead was uncertain, the dangers real. But I was ready. We were ready. For the first time in a long time, I felt a spark of hope. We were stronger together, and together, we would bring Victor down. No matter the cost.

9

Chloe

The air was thick with tension as we approached the heart of Victor's empire. Every step felt heavy, like walking through a dream where the ground could give way at any moment. My pulse raced, my mind a whirl of anger, fear, and a grim determination.

The plan was clear—confront Victor, expose his crimes, and end his reign of terror. But nothing could prepare me for the emotions that roiled within me as we closed in on him.

The room we entered was opulent, a stark contrast to the horrors Victor had orchestrated.

The walls were lined with expensive art, the furniture lavish and carefully arranged.

It was a facade of civility, masking the darkness that lay beneath. Victor stood at the centre, a calm smile playing on his lips as if he were expecting us.

Seeing him there, so composed and unrepentant, ignited a fire in me. This was the man who had destroyed so many lives, who had taken everything from me.

"Chloe," he greeted, his voice smooth and sickeningly familiar. His eyes flicked to Adrian, and I could see the calculation in his gaze, the way he weighed the situation. "And Adrian. I must say, I didn't expect you to come together."

I felt Adrian's steady presence beside me, a silent pillar of strength. It was grounding, knowing he was there, that we were in this together. But as Victor's gaze locked onto mine, a flood of memories came rushing back—memories of the life we once had, of the lies he told, and the love I thought we shared. It was a painful reminder of how deeply he'd betrayed me, and it fuelled my anger.

"You sick bastard," I spat, my voice trembling with rage. "All those people, those lives you destroyed. Did you ever feel a shred of remorse? Or was it all just a game to you?"

Victor's smile widened; his eyes gleaming with a perverse kind of delight. "Oh, Chloe," he said, his tone mocking. "So much passion. It's almost endearing. But you must understand, this is business. Nothing personal."

His words stung, a cold reminder of his complete lack of empathy. But I couldn't let him get to me. This wasn't about our past, or the twisted relationship we once had. This was about justice. About making him pay for every heinous act he'd committed.

I took a step forward, my hands clenched into fists. "You call this business?" I snarled, my voice rising. "Trafficking innocent people, exploiting them for your gain? You're a monster, Victor."

Before I could react, Victor's expression darkened, a flicker of something dangerous in his eyes. He took a step towards me, his posture menacing.

But before he could do anything, Adrian was there, moving between us. His presence was like a shield, a barrier between me and the man who had caused so much pain.

"Back off," Adrian warned, his voice cold and steady. His hand hovered near his gun, ready to act if necessary. "You don't get to intimidate her anymore."

For a moment, the room was silent, the tension thick and suffocating. Victor's gaze flicked between us, assessing the situation. I could see the wheels turning in his mind, the calculation of risk and reward. But he underestimated us, underestimated the strength of our resolve.

Victor's eyes narrowed, and I could see the mask slipping, revealing the cold, calculating man beneath.

"You think you can stop me?" he sneered. "You're just a couple of disgraced nobodies. You don't have the power to bring me down."

His words hit like a punch, but I refused to back down. Adrian and I exchanged a glance, a silent understanding passing between us. We were in this together, and we wouldn't let Victor win. Not this time.

***

Adrian

The tension in the room was palpable, a thick, oppressive force that seemed to press in from all sides. I kept my eyes on Victor, watching for any sign of movement, any indication that he might try something.

My hand rested lightly on the grip of my gun, a silent warning that I was ready to act if necessary. But even as I focused on the immediate threat, I couldn't ignore the torrent of emotions churning within me.

Seeing Chloe confront Victor was a visceral experience. Her anger, her pain—it was all laid bare, raw and unfiltered. She was fierce, unyielding, a force to be reckoned with. It was a side of her I'd always admired, her strength and determination. But it was also heartbreaking, a reminder of everything she'd lost because of this man.

Victor's eyes flicked to me, a calculating look in his gaze. He was dangerous, and I knew better than to underestimate him. But as I looked into his cold, emotionless eyes, I felt a surge of protectiveness.

For Chloe, for the people he'd hurt. For everyone who'd suffered because of his greed and cruelty.

"You have no idea what you're dealing with," Victor said, his voice dripping with disdain. "You think you can just walk in here and take me down? You're playing a dangerous game, Adrian."

I met his gaze, unflinching. "We're not playing games," I replied, my voice steady. "We're here to end this. To end you."

For a moment, Victor seemed to hesitate, a flicker of uncertainty crossing his features. But then his expression hardened, a cold smile curling his lips. "You're both fools," he said, his tone venomous. "Do you really think you can win? I've built an empire. I've got connections, resources. You can't touch me."

His arrogance was infuriating, but I refused to let it get to me. This was the moment we'd been waiting for, the culmination of all our efforts. We couldn't let him shake us, couldn't let him win.

I felt Chloe's hand slip into mine, a small, comforting gesture that sent a jolt of warmth through me. It was a reminder that we weren't alone, that we had each other.

As Victor continued to spew his vitriol, I tightened my grip on Chloe's hand, drawing strength from her presence. The plan was clear: we had to corner him, force him to confess, and get the evidence we needed to bring him down. But as I looked into her eyes, I saw something else—a spark of desire, and an idea.

Without thinking, I pulled her closer, our bodies pressing together. The world around us seemed to fade away, the tension and danger momentarily forgotten.

Our eyes locked, and in that instant, the anger, the fear, the confusion—it all melted away. All that mattered was the connection between us, the unspoken bond that had been growing stronger with each passing moment.

Before I could stop myself, I leaned in, capturing her lips in a fierce, passionate kiss. It was a release, a way of expressing everything I couldn't put into words. The kiss was desperate, hungry, filled with all the pent-up emotions we'd been holding back. Chloe responded with equal fervour, her hands tangling in my hair as she pulled me closer.

For a moment, it was just us—lost in the intensity of the moment, in the raw, unfiltered desire that pulsed between us. But then, reality came crashing back in, our trick way to victor. Victor's mocking laughter cut through the haze, a harsh reminder of where we were and what we were up against.

I pulled back, my breath ragged, my heart pounding. Chloe looked equally flustered, her cheeks flushed, her eyes dark with emotion. But there was no time to dwell on what had just happened. We had a job to do as our plan.

Victor's gaze was cold, a twisted smile playing on his lips. "Touching," he sneered, his voice dripping with sarcasm. "A touching display of affection. But it won't save you."

He reached into his pocket, and for a split second, I thought he might be reaching for a

weapon. My hand tightened on my gun, ready to act. But instead, he pulled out a phone, holding it up for us to see. My stomach dropped as I realized what he was doing.

"You're too late," Victor said, his voice cold and confident. "I've already made arrangements. Even if you kill me, my operation will continue. You can't stop it."

My mind raced, trying to process what he was saying. He was bluffing, he had to be. But the look in his eyes, the certainty in his voice—it was unnerving.

Chloe's hand tightened in mine, and I felt her fear, her uncertainty. But I couldn't let it show. We had to stay strong, had to believe we could win.

"We'll see about that," I said, my voice firm. "We're not leaving here without you. One way or another, this ends tonight."

Victor's smile widened, a chilling, malevolent grin. "Then let's see how it plays out," he said, his voice low and menacing. "But remember this,

Adrian: you're just a pawn in a much bigger game. And in the end, the house always wins."

As his words hung in the air, I felt a surge of determination. Victor was dangerous, but he wasn't invincible. We had come too far, sacrificed too much to back down now. And no matter what, I would protect Chloe. I would protect us.

The confrontation was far from over, and the danger was real. But as I looked into Chloe's eyes, I knew one thing for certain: we were stronger together. And together, we would bring Victor down. No matter what it took.

And we did it.

10

Chloe

The aftermath of Victor's arrest felt like being caught in the eye of a storm. One moment, we were pulling off a daring rescue and confrontation, and the next, we were thrust into the blinding glare of the public eye.

The world seemed to explode around us, a cacophony of flashing cameras, shouted questions, and the relentless scrutiny of the media. I had known this would happen, but nothing could have prepared me for the reality of it.

The courthouse steps were swarming with reporters, their microphones thrust forward like weapons. They called out my name, their voices blending into a chaotic symphony that filled the air. The questions came rapid-fire, each one more invasive than the last.

"Chloe Laurent, how does it feel to be back in the spotlight?"

"Were you involved in Victor's crimes?"

"Are you trying to redeem yourself?"

The accusations, the insinuations—they cut deep. Even as I tried to focus on the positive, on the fact that Victor was finally in custody, it was impossible to ignore the sting of the public's judgment.

To some, I would always be the disgraced art dealer, the woman who had fallen from grace. No matter what I did, no matter how many lives I tried to save, there would always be those who doubted me, who saw only my mistakes.

I clenched my fists at my sides, my nails digging into my palms. The pressure was suffocating, a weight pressing down on my chest. I wanted to scream, to shout at them to leave me alone. But I knew that would only make things worse. I had to keep my composure, had to maintain the image of strength and control.

Adrian was by my side, his presence a steadying force amidst the chaos. He reached out, gently placing a hand on the small of my back.

It was a subtle gesture, but it grounded me, reminded me that I wasn't alone in this. I glanced at him, meeting his eyes. There was a softness there, a silent promise that he would be with me every step of the way.

We pushed through the crowd, making our way to the waiting car. The reporters continued to shout questions, their voices a relentless barrage. But I blocked them out, focusing on the warmth of Adrian's hand, the strength of his support. It was a small comfort, but it was enough to keep me from breaking.

Once we were safely inside the car, the doors closed, and the noise faded to a dull roar outside. I let out a breath I hadn't realized I'd been holding, my shoulders sagging with the weight of it all. The silence inside the car was a stark contrast to the chaos outside, a moment of reprieve in the eye of the storm.

Adrian turned to me; concern etched on his face. "Are you okay?" he asked, his voice soft, a quiet rumble that cut through the tension.

I nodded, but the truth was, I wasn't sure. Everything felt so overwhelming, so out of control. I felt like I was drowning, struggling to keep my head above water. The fear, the doubt, the guilt—it all crashed over me in waves, threatening to pull me under.

Adrian seemed to sense my turmoil. Without a word, he reached out and took my hand, his touch gentle but firm. He pulled me closer, his arm wrapping around my shoulders in a comforting embrace. I leaned into him, closing my eyes as I rested my head against his chest.

His heartbeat was steady, a soothing rhythm that helped calm the storm inside me.

"It's going to be okay," he murmured, his lips brushing against my temple. "We'll get through this. Together."

The warmth of his words, the certainty in his voice—it was like a lifeline, pulling me back from

the brink. I felt a tear slip down my cheek, and I quickly wiped it away, embarrassed by the show of emotion. But Adrian didn't let go. Instead, he tilted my chin up, his eyes locking onto mine.

"Hey," he whispered, his voice tender. "It's okay to let it out. You don't have to be strong all the time."

His words were like a balm to my wounded soul. For so long, I'd felt like I had to carry the weight of the world on my shoulders, like I couldn't afford to show any weakness. But here, with Adrian, I felt safe. I felt seen.

Without thinking, I leaned in and kissed him. It wasn't a passionate kiss, but a soft, tender one, filled with gratitude and vulnerability. Adrian responded in kind, his lips gentle against mine. It was a moment of connection, a shared acknowledgment of the pain and uncertainty we were both feeling. It was also a promise—that no matter what happened, we would face it together

As we pulled away, Adrian cupped my cheek, his thumb brushing away a tear. "We'll get through this," he repeated, his voice firm and reassuring. "No matter what."

I nodded, feeling a flicker of hope amidst the darkness. It wasn't going to be easy. There would be challenges, doubts, and moments of fear. But as long as we had each other, I knew we could face whatever came our way.

The car started moving, the city lights flashing by outside the window. I leaned back, resting my head on Adrian's shoulder. The road ahead was uncertain, filled with unknowns.

But for the first time in a long time, I felt a sense of peace. We had made it this far, and we would keep fighting. For justice, for redemption, and for the chance at a future free from the shadows of our past.

11

Adrian

The offer had come unexpectedly, like a ghost from a past life. My old MI6 contact, Daniel, had reached out, asking to meet in a nondescript bar on the outskirts of the city. As I walked through the door, the dim lighting and familiar scent of whiskey brought back a flood of memories. It was a place I'd frequented during my years with the agency, a haven for quiet conversations and clandestine meetings. Now, it felt like a relic of a bygone era.

Daniel was waiting in a booth at the back, a glass of scotch in hand. He looked the same as always—calm, composed, with a hint of the enigmatic aura that had made him such an effective spy. As I approached, he gestured for me to sit, a small smile playing on his lips.

"Adrian," he greeted, his voice smooth and steady. "It's been a while."

I nodded, settling into the seat across from him. "It has," I replied, my tone guarded. "What brings you here?"

He took a sip of his drink, his eyes never leaving mine. "I heard about your recent activities," he said, a hint of amusement in his voice. "Impressive work, taking down Victor. MI6 could use someone like you back in the fold."

The offer hung in the air, heavy with implications. For a moment, I was tempted. The thrill of espionage, the sense of purpose—it had been my life for so long. But as I looked at Daniel, I felt a pang of unease. The world of secrets and lies, of constant danger and uncertainty, no longer held the same allure.

"I appreciate the offer," I said slowly, choosing my words carefully. "But I've moved on. My life is... different now."

Daniel raised an eyebrow, clearly intrigued. "Different how?" he asked, leaning forward slightly. "You were one of our best agents, Adrian. You can't tell me you don't miss it."

I hesitated, my mind flashing back to the events of the past few months. The mission, the danger, the relentless pursuit of justice—it had felt like stepping back into a familiar role. But then there was Chloe. Her fierce determination, her vulnerability, the way she challenged me and made me feel alive in a way I hadn't in years. Being with her had changed me, forced me to confront parts of myself I'd long buried.

"I've found something else," I admitted, my voice quiet. "Someone, actually. And she's... she's everything to me."

Daniel studied me for a moment, his expression inscrutable. "This woman," he said slowly. "She's the reason you won't come back?"

I nodded, the truth settling in my chest like a warm, reassuring weight. "Yes," I replied, meeting his gaze. "I can't go back to that life. Not now. Not with her."

He leaned back, his expression softening. "You know, love and espionage don't usually mix," he remarked, a hint of a smile tugging at his lips.

"But if anyone could make it work, I suppose it's you."

We talked for a while longer, exchanging stories and catching up on old times. But as the night wore on, I knew my decision was final. The life I'd once known was behind me, and I was ready to embrace whatever lay ahead. With Chloe.

The drive back to the safe house was quiet, the weight of the conversation still lingering in my mind.

As I pulled into the driveway, I felt a sense of calm wash over me. The house was dark, the only light coming from a single window upstairs. Chloe was waiting for me.

I entered quietly, not wanting to disturb the peace of the night. But as I climbed the stairs and reached the bedroom, I found Chloe sitting on the edge of the bed, her eyes bright and alert. She looked up as I entered, her expression a mix of curiosity and concern.

"How did it go?" she asked, her voice soft but laced with tension.

I hesitated for a moment, then crossed the room to stand in front of her. "They want me back," I said simply. "MI6."

Her eyes widened slightly, a flicker of fear crossing her features. "And what did you say?" she asked, her voice barely above a whisper.

I reached out, gently cupping her face in my hands. "I told them no," I said, my voice firm. "I told them I have something more important now. Someone more important."

She looked up at me, her eyes searching mine. "Are you sure?" she asked, her voice trembling. "I don't want you to give up everything for me."

I smiled, brushing a strand of hair away from her face. "It's not giving up," I replied, leaning down to press a soft kiss to her lips. "It's choosing what matters most."

She sighed against my lips, her hands sliding up to rest on my shoulders. The kiss deepened, a slow, tender exploration that spoke of all the emotions we couldn't put into words. It was a moment of connection, a reaffirmation of our commitment to each other.

As the kiss intensified, I felt a surge of desire, a need to be close to her, to feel her warmth and presence. I pulled her closer, my hands roaming over her back, her waist. She responded eagerly, her fingers tangling in my hair as I pulled her down onto the bed.

The room was filled with the sound of our breathing, the rustle of clothes as we shed the barriers between us. Every touch, every kiss was electric, a reminder of the passion that burned between us.

I felt her body arch beneath me, her skin warm and soft against mine. It was intoxicating, the way she responded to my touch, the way her breath hitched as I explored the contours of her body.

I leaned down, capturing her lips in another deep kiss. She moaned softly, her hands gripping my shoulders as she pulled me closer.

The world outside faded away, leaving only the two of us, lost in the intensity of the moment. It was a dance of desire and need, a physical manifestation of the love and trust we had built.

As we moved together, I felt a sense of completeness, a feeling that this was where I belonged. Not in the shadows of espionage, but here, with her. It was a realization that filled me with a deep, abiding joy, a certainty that I had found my place in the world.

Afterwards, we lay together, our bodies intertwined, the warmth of our shared intimacy lingering in the air. Chloe rested her head on my chest, her fingers tracing lazy patterns on my skin. I held her close, feeling the steady rise and fall of her breath, the gentle rhythm of her heartbeat.

For a long moment, we lay in comfortable silence, content to simply be in each other's presence. But eventually, Chloe shifted, propping herself up on one elbow to look at me.

There was a softness in her eyes, a vulnerability that made my heart ache.

"Adrian," she murmured, her voice barely above a whisper. "Are you sure about this? About us?"

I reached up, gently cupping her cheek. "Surer than I've ever been," I replied, my voice steady. "You mean everything to me, Chloe. I want to build a life with you. A future. No more secrets, no more lies."

She smiled, a radiant, genuine smile that made my heart soar. "I want that too," she said softly, leaning down to press a gentle kiss to my lips. "I want it more than anything."

We kissed again, a slow, lingering kiss that held the promise of a future filled with love and hope. As we pulled away, I held her close, feeling a sense of peace settle over me. The path ahead was uncertain, filled with challenges and unknowns. But with Chloe by my side, I knew we could face anything. Together.

12

Chloe

The email had arrived early in the morning, nestled among the usual array of junk mail and newsletters. At first, I nearly deleted it without a second thought, but something about the sender's name caught my eye. James Caldwell. A prominent figure in the art world, known for his prestigious galleries and a keen eye for talent. My heart raced as I opened the message, curiosity piqued and cautious optimism bubbling beneath the surface.

The offer was clear and concise: an opportunity to restart my career as an art dealer, with a clean slate. Caldwell was willing to vouch for me, to help me rebuild my reputation and establish myself anew. It was everything I had ever wanted, a chance to step back into the world I loved and prove that I was more than the mistakes of my past. But, as always, there were conditions.

The message laid them out plainly: public appearances, interviews, and a willingness to discuss my history. It was a double-edged sword. On one hand, it was a chance to clear my name, to tell my side of the story.

On the other, it meant reopening old wounds, facing the relentless scrutiny of the media, and reliving the most painful moments of my life.

I sat at the kitchen table, the tablet in my hands feeling suddenly heavy. The house was quiet, the morning sunlight filtering through the curtains and casting a warm glow over the room.

Yet, despite the tranquillity, my mind was a whirlwind of conflicting emotions. The thought of stepping back into the public eye made my stomach churn, memories of the harsh judgment and accusations still fresh in my mind.

I needed to talk to Adrian. He had always been my anchor, the one person who could help me navigate the stormy seas of my emotions. I found him in the living room, reclining on the couch with a book in hand. He looked up as I entered, a soft smile gracing his lips.

"Hey," he greeted, closing the book and setting it aside. "You look deep in thought. What's on your mind?"

I hesitated, unsure of how to begin. But the concern in his eyes, the gentle warmth of his gaze, gave me the courage to speak. I sat down beside him, taking a deep breath before handing him the tablet. He skimmed the email, his expression growing serious as he read.

"James Caldwell," he mused, looking up at me. "That's a big deal, Chloe. He's offering you a real chance here."

I nodded, my hands twisting nervously in my lap. "I know," I murmured, my voice barely above a whisper. "Honestly, I don't know" I admitted, wrapping my arms around myself.

"I'm scared, Adrian. Scared of what people will say, scared of being judged all over again. What if... what if I can't handle it? and the conditions... I'm afraid, what if people still see me as the woman who was involved with Victor? What if they never let me move on?"

He reached out, pulling me into his arms. His embrace was warm and comforting, a safe haven amidst the storm of uncertainty. I buried my face in his chest, inhaling his familiar scent, and felt some of the tension in my body ease.

"You don't have to decide right now," he murmured, pressing a soft kiss to the top of my head. "Take your time. Think it over. Whatever you choose, I'll support you." He said, taking my hands in his.

His touch was warm and reassuring, grounding me in the moment. "People can be cruel," he acknowledged, his voice gentle but firm. "But they can also be forgiving. This is your chance to tell your story, to show them who you really are."

I sighed, leaning back against the couch. "But what if it's not enough?" I asked, my voice wavering. "What if they just see me as a pariah, as someone trying to escape her past?"

Adrian squeezed my hands, his eyes locking onto mine. "Then you show them that you're more than your past," he said softly. "You've already proven that to me. And to yourself. Now, it's time to prove it to the world."

His words stirred something within me, a spark of hope amidst the darkness of doubt. But the fear lingered, a shadow that refused to be chased away. "What if it all goes wrong?" I whispered; my voice barely audible. "What if I can't handle the pressure?"

Adrian's expression softened, and he leaned in, pressing a tender kiss to my forehead. "You can handle anything," he murmured, his lips brushing against my skin. "And you won't have to do it alone. I'm here, Chloe. Always."

The warmth of his words, the sincerity in his voice, wrapped around me like a comforting embrace. I felt a tear slip down my cheek, quickly followed by another.

 Adrian reached up, gently wiping them away with his thumb, then traced his thumb over my lips, slowly exploring, feeling and tenderly caressing. He leaned in closer, his lips hovering just above mine.

"Whatever you decide," he whispered, "I'll be with you every step of the way."

His words brought a swell of emotion to my chest, a mixture of gratitude and love. I reached up, cupping his face in my hands, and kissed him. It was a soft, tender kiss, filled with all the unspoken feelings between us. He responded immediately, his arms tightening around me, pulling me closer.

He Capturing my lips in a soft, lingering kiss. It was a kiss of reassurance, of unspoken promises and unwavering support. His arms wrapped around me, pulling me closer as the kiss deepened, a slow, tender exploration that spoke of the depth of our connection.

He kisses deepened, growing more passionate. I felt the familiar heat of desire ignite between us, a spark that quickly turned into a flame.

My hands roamed over his chest, feeling the hard muscles beneath his shirt. He groaned softly, his fingers tangling in my hair as he tilted my head back, deepening the kiss.

His hands moved with a sense of urgency, quickly unbuttoning my blouse and slipping it off my shoulders. I shivered as the cool air brushed against my skin, feeling a thrill of anticipation.

His hands were warm, his touch gentle as he caressed my bare skin, sending shivers down my spine.

We moved together, a familiar dance of need and want. His hands slid down my back, pulling me closer, pressing me against the solid wall of his body. I could feel his heartbeat, strong and steady, matching the rhythm of my own. Our thumping heartbeats, leaving only the two of us in the moment.

When we pulled away, I rested my forehead against his chest, our breaths mingling in the space between us. "I love you," I whispered, the words slipping out before I could stop them.

It was the first time I had told him, the first time I had allowed myself to fully acknowledge the depth of my feelings.

Adrian smiled, a soft, genuine smile that made my heart ache with joy. "I love you too," he

replied, his voice filled with warmth and certainty. "And whatever happens, we'll face it together."

He kissed me again, a searing kiss that left me breathless.

our kisses becoming more frantic, more desperate. He pushed me down onto the couch hard every time, his body covering mine. I felt his weight, his touch, and it was intoxicating. I reached up. Pulling him closer. needing to feel every inch of him. He moved as if in need to devour me. He moved to dive deeper in me.

The world outside ceased to exist as we made love, a passionate and intense joining that left us both breathless. It was a moment of pure connection, a merging of bodies and souls. I felt safe in his arms, protected from the chaos and uncertainty of the world outside. With him, I felt whole.

Afterwards, we lay together, our bodies tangled with each other. The room was filled with the soft sound of our breathing, a gentle reminder of the intimacy we had just shared. I rested my head on his chest, listening to the steady beat of his heart. It was a comforting sound and steady rhythm that grounded me.

He stroked my hair, his touch gentle and soothing. "Whatever you decide," he murmured, his voice soft. "I'll be with you. We can face it together."

I looked up at him. "Thank you," I whispered, leaning up to kiss him softly. "For everything."

He smiled, a warm, genuine smile that made my heart flutter. "You don't have to thank me," he replied, his voice filled with tenderness. "I'm just glad I found you."

As we lay there, wrapped in each other's arms, I felt a sense of peace settle over me. The future was uncertain, filled with challenges and unknowns. But with Adrian by my side, I knew I could face whatever came our way. Together, we could build a new life, a new future. And that was all that mattered.

We were there in silence for a moment, the weight of the decision still heavy in the air. But with Adrian by my side, the fear seemed more manageable, the uncertainty less daunting. We had faced so much together, overcome so many

obstacles. Whatever the future held, I knew we could handle it.

As the sun continued to rise outside, casting its golden light into the room, I felt a sense of peace settle over me. The crossroads before me were daunting, the path uncertain. But with Adrian's love and support, I knew I could face whatever challenges lay ahead. We had each other, and that was enough.

13

Chloe

The courtroom was stifling, a tense silence hanging in the air like a thick fog. I sat at the witness stand, my palms damp with sweat, heart pounding in my chest. The room was filled with spectators, journalists, and legal professionals, all awaiting the trial's most anticipated moment. Victor's trial. The moment when justice would finally catch up with the man who had wreaked havoc on so many lives, including mine.

As the prosecutor began to question me, I took a deep breath, reminding myself to stay composed. I glanced over at Adrian, seated in the audience. He gave me a small, reassuring smile, and I felt a surge of strength. This was it. The moment we had been fighting for.

"Miss Laurent," the prosecutor began, "can you describe your relationship with the defendant, Victor Williams?"

I swallowed hard; my throat dry. "Victor and I were involved in a romantic relationship," I replied, keeping my voice steady. "But it quickly became clear that he was not the man he appeared to be. He manipulated and controlled me, using my career as an art dealer to further his own criminal activities."

As I recounted the events, the courtroom seemed to fade away, replaced by memories of a time I had tried to forget. The glamorous galas, the stolen art, the lies and deceit. It all came rushing back, a tidal wave of emotions threatening to overwhelm me. But I pressed on, determined to expose the truth.

The prosecutor asked about the human trafficking ring, and I felt a chill run down my spine. "Victor used his connections in the art world as a front," I explained, my voice trembling slightly. "He trafficked vulnerable women, exploiting them for his own gain. I had no idea what was happening until it was too late."

As I spoke, I noticed Victor watching me, his expression cold and unyielding. There was a moment, a brief flicker of recognition, as our eyes met. It was a reminder of the hold he once had over me, the power he wielded with such ease. But now, sitting in that courtroom, I felt a sense of liberation. The truth was out, and there was nothing he could do to silence me.

The defence attorney's cross-examination was brutal. He tried to paint me as a scorned lover, someone seeking revenge. But I held my ground, refusing to let him undermine my testimony. The prosecutor's objections were frequent, and at one point, the judge admonished the defence attorney for badgering me. It was a small victory, but it felt significant.

When my testimony was over, I stepped down from the stand, my legs feeling like jelly. As I went to my place to sit Adrian stood up, his hand gently resting on my back as we walked out of the courtroom together. "You did great," he whispered, a hint of pride in his voice. "I'm proud of you."

I managed a small smile, my nerves still frayed. "Thanks," I murmured. "I'm just glad it's over."

He chuckled, a rare sound that brought a spark of warmth to my chest. "Not quite," he said, glancing back at the courtroom. "We've still got Victor's testimony to sit through. And my own, of course."

I sighed, feeling a mix of exhaustion and relief. "Let's just get it over with," I replied, leaning against him for support. "And maybe, when this is all done, we can finally go somewhere sunny and forget about all this."

Adrian grinned, a mischievous glint in his eye. "How about a remote island with no Wi-Fi?" he suggested. "Just you, me, and a bunch of coconuts. We can reenact Castaway."

I couldn't help but laugh, the tension in my shoulders easing slightly. "As long as you promise not to make friends with a volleyball," I teased, feeling a bit lighter.

He gave me a mock-serious look. "No promises," he said, then added with a smirk, "But I'll try to stick to human company."

***

Adrian

Watching Chloe testify was like seeing a phoenix rise from the ashes. She had faced down Victor with a courage that left me in awe, her words cutting through the lies and deception like a blade. It was a testament to her strength, her resilience. But now, it was my turn.

As I took the stand, I felt the weight of the courtroom's eyes on me. The prosecutor's questions were direct, focusing on my involvement with MI6 and the mission that had led to Victor's downfall. I recounted the events with precision, detailing the operation, the intelligence we had gathered, and the eventual takedown of Victor's network.

The prosecutor then shifted focus. "Mr. Bennett, can you describe the nature of your relationship with the defendant, Victor Williams?"

I nodded, taking a moment to gather my thoughts. "Victor was a high-value target," I explained. "He was involved in multiple illegal activities, including art theft and human trafficking. My mission was to infiltrate his organization and gather evidence to dismantle it."

The defence attorney was relentless in his cross-examination, trying to poke holes in my testimony. He questioned my methods, implying that I had acted outside the bounds of the law. But I remained composed, countering his accusations with facts and evidence. The judge had to intervene several times, warning the defence attorney to stick to the facts.

Finally, the defence attorney leaned in, his voice dripping with scepticism. "Mr. Bennett, isn't it true that you were motivated by personal feelings towards Miss Laurent, rather than a professional duty to your country?"

I felt a surge of anger but kept my expression neutral. "My feelings for Chloe had nothing to do with my duty," I said evenly. "I was doing my job, gathering evidence to stop a dangerous criminal. The fact that Chloe was caught in the crossfire only made me more determined to bring Victor to justice."

As I stepped down from the stand, I glanced at Chloe, who gave me a small, encouraging nod. We walked out of the courtroom together, the weight of the trial hanging heavily over us. But there was a sense of closure, a feeling that we were finally putting the past behind us.

Outside the courtroom, the media swarmed, cameras flashing and reporters shouting questions. It was overwhelming, the noise and chaos a stark contrast to the quiet intensity of the trial. But amidst the frenzy, I caught Chloe's eye, and we shared a knowing look. We had faced the worst together, and we had come out the other side stronger.

As we navigated out of the crowd, I leaned in close to Chloe, my lips brushing against her ear. "You know," I whispered, "once this is all over, we should seriously consider that island idea. Just you, me, and a lifetime supply of coconut water."

She laughed, a genuine, carefree sound that made my heart swell. "Sounds like a plan," she replied, a playful twinkle in her eye. "As long as you promise not to wear a loincloth."

I grinned, pulling her close for a quick, mischievous kiss. "No loincloth, but I can't make any promises about coconut bras," I teased, enjoying the light-hearted banter.

She rolled her eyes, but her smile was radiant. "Deal," she said, her voice warm and full of affection. "Now, let's get out of here before they start asking for autographs."

As we made our way to our car, I felt a sense of relief wash over me. The trial was coming to an end, and with it, a chapter of our lives that had been filled with pain and uncertainty.

But now, we were ready to start anew, to build a future together. And no matter what challenges lay ahead, I knew we could face them. Because we had each other, and that was all we needed.

14

Chloe

The days following the trial were a whirlwind. The courtroom drama had finally ended, and Victor was behind bars, facing the consequences of his actions.

Yet, as the dust settled, I found myself grappling with an unexpected proposition. A publisher had reached out, offering me a lucrative deal to write a tell-all book about my experiences with Victor and the trial that followed.

At first, the idea was both thrilling and terrifying. It was a chance to set the record straight, to tell my side of the story without the media's sensationalism. But it also meant dredging up the past, reliving moments I'd rather forget.

As I sat in our cozy Paris apartment, the city lights twinkling outside the window, I pondered the offer with a mixture of excitement and dread.

Adrian walked in, carrying two mugs of hot chocolate. He had taken to making it every evening, claiming it was the perfect way to wind down after a long day. I couldn't argue; there was something comforting about the rich, warm drink, especially when shared with him.

"Your usual," he said, handing me a mug with a flourish. He was grinning, a mischievous glint in his eyes. "Extra marshmallows, as requested."

I smiled, accepting the mug. "Thank you, kind sir," I replied, taking a sip. The sweetness melted on my tongue, a delicious contrast to the slight chill of the evening air. "Perfect as always."

He settled next to me on the couch, his arm draping casually over my shoulders. For a moment, we sat in comfortable silence, the warmth of his presence a soothing balm to my frazzled nerves. But I knew we couldn't avoid the topic forever.

"So," Adrian began, breaking the silence. "Have you thought anything about the book offer?"

I sighed, setting my mug down on the coffee table. "It's all I've been thinking about," I admitted. "Part of me wants to do it. To finally tell my side of the story and clear my name. But another part of me... I don't know, Adrian. What if it just ties me to the past even more? What if people still see me as 'Victor's ex' instead of who I really am?"

He nodded thoughtfully, his fingers gently tracing patterns on my shoulder. "I get it," he said softly. "It's a big decision. But you know, it could also be a way to move forward. To take control of your narrative and show the world the real Chloe Laurent. Not just the woman they think they know."

His words were comforting, a reminder that I wasn't alone in this. I leaned into him, resting my head against his shoulder. "And what if I decide not to do it?" I asked, my voice barely above a whisper. "Would that make me a coward?"

He tilted his head, looking down at me with a gentle smile. "Choosing not to do it wouldn't make you a coward," he reassured me. "It would just mean you're prioritizing your peace of mind. There's no right or wrong choice here, Chloe. Whatever you decide, it's your decision. Because it's your life, not theirs."

I felt the love I had for him filling my heart. "Thank you," I whispered, lifting my head to meet his gaze. "For always being here for me."

He chuckled, his eyes sparkling with warmth. "Always," he promised, leaning in to kiss me. It was a soft, lingering kiss, a tender affirmation of our bond. As our lips parted, he pulled back slightly, a playful grin spreading across his face. "Besides," he added, "if you write the book, you can include a chapter on how you fell for the ridiculously handsome ex-MI6 agent."

I laughed, rolling my eyes. "Oh, really?" I teased, poking him in the side. "And what would that chapter be titled? 'How to Deal with a Painfully Modest Boyfriend'?"

He feigned a hurt expression, placing a hand over his heart. "Ouch, Chloe," he said, his tone mock-serious. "You're wounding my delicate ego."

I couldn't help but giggle, the tension easing from my shoulders. "Well, if I do write the book, I promise to include a special dedication to you," I said, a smile playing on my lips. "For being the best marshmallow supplier and for putting up with me."

He grinned, leaning in to plant a quick kiss on my lips. "I'll hold you to that," he said, his voice low and playful.

As the night wore on, we continued to talk about the book, the possibilities, and the potential pitfalls. Adrian shared his thoughts, his insights both practical and encouraging.

We laughed about the absurdity of the media's portrayal of our lives and joked about the outrageous stories we could fabricate if we ever wanted to mess with the public.

But beneath the humour and light-hearted banter, there was a deep, unspoken understanding. This decision wasn't just about the book; it was about reclaiming my life, my identity. And Adrian, with his unwavering support, was a constant reminder that I had the strength to do so.

In the end, I decided to write the book. But on my terms. It wouldn't be a sensationalized tell-all; it would be a story of resilience and healing.

A story about finding myself amidst the chaos and learning to let go of the past. Adrian would be a part of it, not as a footnote in my story, but as a central figure who helped me find my way back to myself.

As we finished our hot chocolate and the night grew late, I felt a sense of peace settle over me. The future was uncertain, but for the first time in a long time, I felt ready to face it. With Adrian by my side, I knew I could handle whatever came our way. And together, we would write the next chapter of our lives, one filled with love, laughter, and endless possibilities.

15

Adrian

The early morning sun cast a warm, golden glow over the cobblestone streets of Paris as Chloe and I walked hand in hand through the quiet alleys. The city, usually buzzing with life, felt oddly serene in the early hours.

It was as if Paris itself was bidding us a gentle farewell. Our bags were packed, tickets ready, and our hearts filled with a mix of excitement and uncertainty. We were leaving Paris, setting off on a journey across Europe, a journey to rediscover ourselves and each other.

As we boarded the train, I couldn't help but feel a sense of relief wash over me. The past few months had been a whirlwind of emotions, filled with danger, courtroom battles, and difficult decisions. But now, as the train chugged along the tracks, leaving the familiar skyline of Paris behind, I felt a newfound sense of freedom. It was as if a weight had been lifted off my shoulders, a weight I hadn't even realized I was carrying.

Chloe leaned her head on my shoulder, her eyes closed as she relaxed into the rhythm of the train. I watched her, a small smile playing on my lips. She looked peaceful; her face softened in the gentle light streaming through the window. It was a far cry from the tense, guarded woman I had first met. She had been through so much, but she had emerged stronger, more resilient. And I admired her all the more for it.

Our journey took us through the picturesque countryside, past rolling hills and charming villages. We stopped at small towns, exploring their winding streets, sampling local delicacies, and immersing ourselves in the simple pleasures of life. It was a far cry from the chaos of my former profession, a life filled with espionage, danger, and secrets. For the first time in years, I felt free. Free from the burdens of my past, free to be myself, and free to love Chloe without reservation.

In a quaint village nestled in the hills of Provence, we found a cozy little inn run by an elderly couple. The inn was charming, with its ivy-covered walls and flower-filled courtyard. We settled into our room, the rustic decor adding to the charm. As we unpacked, Chloe pulled out a small map, spreading it out on the bed.

"Where to next?" she asked, her eyes sparkling with excitement.

I shrugged, a grin spreading across my face. "Wherever the wind takes us," I replied, enjoying the spontaneity of our adventure. "We've got no set plans, remember?"

She laughed, the sound like music to my ears. "Right, no plans," she said, leaning over the map.

"But I was thinking... Italy? I've always wanted to see the Amalfi Coast."

I raised an eyebrow, intrigued. "Italy, huh? Sounds perfect," I said, pulling her close. "But for now, how about we explore this little village? Maybe find a quiet spot for lunch, just the two of us?"

She nodded, her smile widening. "I'd like that," she agreed, wrapping her arms around me. "Just you and me, no distractions."

We spent the day wandering through the village, exploring its hidden corners and discovering little gems along the way. We found a small cafe tucked away in a side street, where we sat outside, enjoying the sunshine and a delicious meal. The cafe owner, a jovial man with a thick accent, regaled us with stories of the village's history, his animated gestures making us laugh.

As the sun began to set, casting a warm glow over the village, we made our way to a small hill overlooking the valley. The view was breathtaking, the landscape bathed in the golden hues of dusk. We sat down on a blanket, a bottle of wine and two glasses in hand, and watched as the sun dipped below the horizon.

Chloe sighed contentedly, resting her head on my shoulder. "This is perfect," she murmured, her voice soft. "Just us, no drama, no chaos. I could get used to this."

I smiled, placing a gentle kiss on her forehead. "Me too," I agreed, feeling a deep sense of contentment. "It's nice to just... be. No secrets, no missions, just us."

We sat in comfortable silence, the only sounds the gentle rustling of leaves and the distant murmur of the village below. As the stars began to twinkle in the night sky, I turned to Chloe, a thought suddenly occurring to me.

"You know," I began, a playful grin spreading across my face, "we could just keep going. Travel the world, see all the places we've dreamed of. No plans, no schedules, just us and the open road."

Chloe laughed, her eyes sparkling in the dim light. "Sounds like an adventure," she said, her voice filled with excitement. "But what about work, responsibilities, all that grown-up stuff?"

I shrugged, a mischievous glint in my eye. "Work can wait," I replied, leaning in to kiss her. "Responsibilities... well, we can figure those out later. Right now, I just want to enjoy this moment with you."

Our lips met in a tender kiss, the world around us fading away. It was a kiss filled with love, passion, and a promise of a future filled with endless possibilities. As we pulled away, I looked into her eyes, feeling a surge of emotion.

"Chloe," I whispered, my voice filled with sincerity. "I love you. More than anything in this world. And wherever this journey takes us, as long as we're together, I know it'll be worth it."

She smiled, her eyes glistening with unshed tears. "I love you too, Adrian," she replied, her voice barely above a whisper. "You've given me more than I ever thought possible. And I can't wait to see where this journey takes us."

We sat there, wrapped in each other's arms, the stars shining brightly above us. It was a moment of pure bliss, a moment that felt like the beginning of a new chapter in our lives. A chapter filled with love, adventure, and the promise of a beautiful future together. And as we sat there, basking in the warmth of our love, I knew that no matter what the future held, we would face it together, hand in hand.

16

Chloe

The vibrant streets of Positano were a feast for the senses. The scent of lemon trees mingled with the salty sea breeze, and the colourful houses clung to the cliffs, cascading down towards the azure waters.

Italy had always been a dream destination, but being here with Adrian made it all the more magical. We spent our days exploring quaint towns, indulging in exquisite food, and revelling in the beauty of the Amalfi Coast.

It was a welcome escape, a chance to breathe and savour the freedom of anonymity.

One afternoon, as we wandered through a narrow alleyway, we stumbled upon a small art gallery. Its facade was unassuming, with faded blue shutters and a simple sign that read "Arte di Speranza"—Art of Hope. Intrigued, we stepped inside, greeted by the gentle chime of a bell. The gallery was a humble space, filled with vibrant paintings and sculptures, each piece brimming with emotion and raw beauty.

A young woman, no older than twenty, approached us with a warm smile. Her name was Lucia, she told us, and she was one of the artists featured in the gallery. As she spoke about her work, her passion and dedication were palpable.

She explained that the gallery was more than just an art space; it was a sanctuary for victims of human trafficking. The artists here were survivors, using their art as a form of healing and expression.

Lucia's story moved me deeply. She spoke of her journey, how she had been lured into a trafficking ring with false promises and had endured unimaginable horrors. It was only through the help of a local artist, Tom, who ran the gallery, that she had escaped and found a new purpose. Tom, she said, had dedicated his life to helping survivors like her, providing them with shelter, art therapy, and a chance to rebuild their lives.

As Lucia shared her story, I felt a familiar ache in my chest. The past few months had been a whirlwind of emotions, and hearing Lucia's experience brought everything rushing back. The pain, the guilt, the overwhelming desire to make things right. I glanced at Adrian, who listened intently, his jaw clenched with quiet determination. I knew he felt the same way—compelled to help, to use our skills and connections for something greater.

That evening, after we returned to our hotel, Adrian and I sat on the balcony, overlooking the stunning view of the Mediterranean. The sun had just set, casting a soft glow over the horizon. We sat in comfortable silence for a while, both lost in our thoughts. Finally, I broke the silence.

"Adrian," I began, my voice hesitant. "What Lucia said today... it reminded me of everything we've been through. The things we've seen. And I can't help but think... maybe we're meant to do something more. Something meaningful."

He turned to me, his eyes searching mine. "I was thinking the same thing," he admitted, reaching out to take my hand. "We've seen the worst of what people can do to each other. But we've also seen the power of hope and resilience. Maybe it's time we put our pasts to good use."

His words resonated with me, stirring something deep within. The idea of helping survivors, of giving them a voice and a chance at a new life, felt like a calling. It was an opportunity to atone for my past mistakes, to channel my pain into something positive. I squeezed his hand, feeling a surge of determination.

"I want to help," I said, my voice steady. "Whatever it takes, I want to be a part of this. To use my experiences, my connections, to make a difference. And I want to do it with you."

Adrian smiled, a look of pride and affection in his eyes. "Then let's do it," he said, his voice filled with conviction. "Together."

Over the next few days, we met with Marco Lombardi and his fiancée" at the gallery while helping the artist. We discussed about an art piece made by a Thai artist. It is the art piece that Marco wants to gift Yumi as she likes that art piece but artist said that it's not for selling.

We had doubts that Marco wants something and he isn't using his power to get that. But soon we got the answer when Marco said Yumi has strictly said no to violence or power harassment for an art piece.

 So, I decide to assist them as the Thai artist is my long-known friend and I know she wouldn't say no to me. Adrian's background in espionage proved invaluable; he helped them tighten security for their new mansion.

Meanwhile, I worked on using my contacts in the art world to raise awareness and funds for the gallery. It was exhausting but fulfilling work, and for the first time in a long time, I felt a sense of purpose.

One evening, after a long day of meetings and planning, Adrian and I returned to our hotel. We were both tired but exhilarated by the progress we'd made. As we entered our room, Adrian wrapped his arms around me, pulling me close. His touch was warm and comforting, and I leaned into him, savouring the moment.

"We make a pretty good team, don't we?" he murmured, his lips brushing against my ear.

I smiled, turning to face him. "The best," I agreed, gazing up at him. His eyes were soft, filled with love and admiration. I felt a rush of affection, my heart swelling with emotion. In that moment, everything felt right. The chaos of our pasts, the uncertainty of our future—it all faded away, leaving only us, together.

Adrian leaned down, capturing my lips in a tender kiss. It was a slow, gentle kiss, filled with unspoken promises and shared dreams. As our lips moved in sync, I felt a surge of warmth spread through me, a sense of peace and contentment. When we finally pulled away, I rested my forehead against his, our breaths mingling in the quiet of the room.

"I love you," I whispered, my voice barely audible.

"I love you too," he replied, his voice equally soft. He pulled me closer, his arms wrapping around me in a protective embrace. We stood there for a while, holding each other, the world outside fading into insignificance.

As we lay in bed that night, I couldn't help but reflect on how far we'd come. From the darkness of our pasts to the light of our new mission, we'd found a way to turn our pain into something beautiful.

It wasn't always easy, and there were still challenges ahead. But with Adrian by my side, I felt ready to face whatever came our way.

And so, as we drifted off to sleep, our hearts full of hope and love, I knew that this was just the beginning. The beginning of a new chapter, a new adventure. A journey not just to escape our pasts, but to build a future filled with purpose, love, and the promise of a better tomorrow.

17

Chloe

The gentle hum of the espresso machine filled the cozy little cafe, mingling with the soft chatter of customers. It had become our favourite spot in the village, a sanctuary of sorts where Adrian and I could relax and enjoy the simple pleasures of life.

We sat at our usual corner table, sipping cappuccinos and sharing a plate of fresh pastries. The sun streamed in through the large windows, casting a warm, golden glow over everything.

I glanced over at Adrian, who was engrossed in the newspaper, a small smile playing on his lips.

He looked more relaxed than I'd ever seen him, the tension in his shoulders replaced with an easy, contented demeanour.

It was a stark contrast to the man I'd first met, the one haunted by shadows and secrets. Seeing him like this made my heart swell with happiness.

As I nibbled on a croissant, my mind wandered to our recent therapy sessions. It hadn't been easy to confront the demons of our pasts, to lay bare the wounds we'd tried so hard to ignore. But it had been necessary. Together, we'd faced our trauma head-on, discussing everything from the betrayals we'd suffered to the guilt that still lingered. It was a painful process, but it was also healing. For the first time, I felt like we were truly on the path to recovery.

"What's on your mind?" Adrian's voice broke through my thoughts, pulling me back to the present. He folded the newspaper and set it aside, his eyes full of curiosity and warmth.

I smiled, reaching across the table to take his hand. "Just thinking about how far we've come," I admitted. "It's been... a journey, hasn't it?"

He chuckled, squeezing my hand gently. "That's an understatement," he said, his eyes twinkling with amusement. "But yeah, it's been quite the ride. And I wouldn't have it any other way."

I laughed, the sound light and carefree. "Me neither," I agreed. "You know, I was thinking... maybe we should do something to celebrate. Something fun and silly. We've been so focused on work and healing; I think we deserve a little break."

Adrian raised an eyebrow, a mischievous grin spreading across his face. "Fun and silly, huh? Any ideas?"

I pretended to think for a moment, tapping my chin with a finger. "Well," I began, trying to keep a straight face, "we could... I don't know... have a water balloon fight? Or maybe go to a karaoke bar and sing terribly off-key?"

He burst out laughing, the sound so infectious that I couldn't help but join in. "A water balloon fight? Really?" he teased, his eyes sparkling with amusement. "You do realize that I'll win, right?"

I smirked, leaning back in my chair. "Oh, you're on," I challenged, grinning from ear to ear. "Don't underestimate me, Mr. Bennet. I've got some serious water balloon skills."

Adrian shook his head, still chuckling. "Alright, Mrs. Bennett, let's see what you've got," he said, leaning in closer. "But don't say I didn't warn you."

"Wait! Who says I'm Mrs. bennet? I'm still Laurent."

He leans towards me "yes, not yet but you will soon accept that surname."

I looked at side, holding back my smile "you're quite over confident about that. Don't you think so?"

He nods his head in denial. "You accept it or not my love. You're going to give birth to my children that's for sure"

He stands up and inclines towards me. Takes my chin in his hand and kisses me with an ardent, lingering passion.

The rest of the day was filled with laughter and playful banter as we prepared for our impromptu water balloon battle. We gathered supplies from a local shop, filling up dozens of colourful balloons in the courtyard of our inn.

As we pelted each other with water balloons, shrieking and laughing like kids, I felt a sense of joy and freedom that I hadn't felt in a long time. It was a reminder that, despite everything we'd been through, we could still find happiness in the simplest of moments.

Later that evening, as we dried off and warmed up with cups of hot cocoa, we talked about our future. Our new venture, Bennett Securities, was taking shape, and we were excited about the possibilities.

We had already reached out to some of the best hackers, former intelligence officers, and veterans from elite military squads. Our goal was to create a team that could handle the toughest security challenges, from cyber threats to physical protection.

As we sat by the fireplace, cozy in our robes, I felt a sense of peace settle over me. The road ahead was still uncertain, but I knew that with Adrian by my side, we could face anything. And for the first time in a long time, I felt hopeful about the future.

***

Adrian

The day had been perfect—a rare, carefree respite from the weight of our pasts. Chloe had surprised me with her competitive spirit during our water balloon fight, her laughter ringing through the air like music. It was moments like these that reminded me of how much I loved her, how much she had become an essential part of my life.

As the night drew in, we settled into the cozy warmth of our inn. The fire crackled softly, casting a gentle glow over the room. I watched Chloe as she sipped her hot cocoa, her eyes closed in contentment. She looked so peaceful; her features softened by the firelight. It was a stark contrast to the woman who had once been tormented by her past. Seeing her like this made me feel like now I'm alive.

I set my cup down and reached for her hand, pulling her closer. She looked up at me, her eyes shining with warmth and love. "What are you thinking about?" she asked, her voice soft and curious.

I smiled, brushing a strand of hair away from her face. "Just how lucky I am," I replied, my voice filled with sincerity. "To have you, to be here with you. It's more than I ever thought possible."

She smiled, her eyes glistening with emotion. "I'm lucky too," she whispered, leaning in to kiss me. Her lips were warm and sweet, a perfect blend of cocoa and love. A tender kiss with a deep, unspoken love. It was a promise of a future together, a future free from the shadows of our pasts.

As we pulled away, I felt a surge of warmth and contentment. I knew that the road ahead wouldn't be easy, that there would be challenges and obstacles to overcome. But I also knew that with Chloe by my side, we could face anything. We had come so far, and I was determined to build a future that was worthy of her—one filled with love, laughter, and purpose.

The next morning, as the sun rose over the hills, we continued our work on Bennett Securities. We reached out to potential team members, discussing our vision and goals. It was exhilarating to see our plans come to life, to build something from the ground up.

The work was challenging, but it was also rewarding. It felt good to use our skills and experiences for something positive, to help others in need.

One day, as we sat in a small cafe, discussing our plans, Chloe suddenly burst into laughter. I looked at her, puzzled, and she pointed at the menu. "Look at this," she said, giggling. "They have a dish called 'Pasta alla Adrian'! Maybe it's a sign!"

I couldn't help but laugh along with her, the sound of her laughter so infectious. "I guess they know talent when they see it," I joked, winking at her. "Should we order it and see if it lives up to the name?"

She grinned, nodding eagerly. "Definitely," she said, her eyes twinkling with mischief. "And if it's terrible, we can blame you."

The pasta turned out to be delicious, much to Chloe's amusement. We spent the rest of the meal making jokes and teasing each other, enjoying the light heartedness of the moment.

It was a reminder that, despite everything, we could still find joy in the little things. And as we walked back to our inn, hand in hand, I knew that we were on the right path.

As the days turned into weeks, our bond grew stronger. We attended therapy together, delving deeper into our past traumas and learning to communicate better. It was a challenging process, but it brought us closer, allowing us to understand each other on a deeper level.

We shared our fears and dreams, our hopes for the future. And through it all, we found a new sense of purpose, a new mission to guide us.

One evening, as we sat on the balcony, watching the sunset, Chloe turned to me, her expression thoughtful. "Do you ever think about the future?" she asked, her voice soft. "About what comes next?"

I nodded, taking her hand in mine. "All the time," I admitted. "I think about the life we could build together, the people we could help, the adventures we could have. And it makes me excited for what's to come."

She smiled; her eyes filled with warmth. "Me too," she said, leaning her head on my shoulder. "Whatever happens, I know we'll face it together. And that's all that matters."

As we sat there, wrapped in each other's arms, I felt a deep sense of peace. We had found each other in the midst of chaos and had emerged stronger, more resilient. And as we continued our journey, I knew that we were ready to embrace whatever the future held, together.

18

Adrian

The day was perfect. The sky was a canvas of blue, with wisps of white clouds lazily drifting by. The sea stretched out endlessly before us, its waves gently lapping against the shore.

The air was crisp, carrying the faint scent of salt and wildflowers.

It was the kind of day that felt like a gift, a reminder of the beauty and serenity that life could offer.

I knew it was the perfect moment to ask Chloe the question that had been on my mind for weeks.

We had spent the afternoon exploring the charming coastal town, wandering through narrow cobblestone streets and admiring the quaint shops and cafes.

 Chloe had been in high spirits, her laughter infectious as she teased me about my lack of knowledge about Italian art.

We had stopped for gelato, savouring the rich, creamy flavours as we strolled along the beach. It was a simple day, filled with simple joys, but it felt like everything was falling into place.

As the sun began to set, painting the sky in hues of orange and pink, I led Chloe to a secluded spot by the cliffs. It was a place we had discovered earlier, a hidden gem with a breathtaking view of the ocean.

The waves crashed against the rocks below, creating a soothing, rhythmic sound that echoed in the quiet evening. We sat down on a blanket, side by side, our hands intertwined.

For a while, we just watched the sunset, the silence between us comfortable and warm. I glanced at Chloe; her profile bathed in the soft, golden light. She looked peaceful; her hair gently tousled by the breeze.

My heart swelled with love and gratitude. She had brought so much light into my life, had stood by me through thick and thin. I knew that I wanted to spend the rest of my life with her.

Taking a deep breath, I reached into my pocket and pulled out the small velvet box. My hands were trembling slightly, but I felt a sense of calm wash over me as I turned to face her. "Chloe," I began, my voice steady, "there's something I need to ask you."

She looked at me, her eyes wide with curiosity and a hint of anticipation. "What is it?" she asked, her voice soft.

Oh god, for me she is gift from heaven. No... she is heaven for me in this chaotic world.

I opened the box, revealing a delicate ring with a single, sparkling diamond. The stone caught the fading light, glinting with a brilliance that matched the love I felt for her.

Chloe gasped, her hand flying to her mouth as she stared at the ring in surprise.

"Chloe Laurent," I said, my voice filled with emotion, "from the moment I met you, my life has been an incredible journey. We've faced so much together—challenges, dangers, and heartaches."

A tear rolled down her cheek as I continued. "But through it all, we've found something beautiful, something worth fighting for. You've shown me what it means to love and be loved, to find strength in vulnerability. You've given me hope, joy, and a sense of purpose."

I paused, my gaze locking with hers. Her eyes were glistening with unshed tears, her expression one of pure, unfiltered emotion. I took her hand in mine, feeling the warmth of her skin against my own.

"I want to spend the rest of my life with you," I continued, my voice barely above a whisper. "To build a future together, to share our dreams, our fears, and our love... Chloe my life, marry me and take my surname as yours."

For a moment, there was silence. The world seemed to stand still as I waited for her response, my heart pounding in my chest. Then, with a soft sob, tears streaming down her cheeks.

 "Is this your order, veteran?" she asked, her voice soft and a gentle smile on her lips.

Getting on my knees, I said, "For you, I'm on my knees and can bring the whole world to your feet, my love."

I took her hand in mine and asked her, "So, would you like to be Mrs. Bennet, Miss Laurent?"

"Yes," she whispered, her voice choked with emotion. "Yes, Adrian, I would be delighted to be your wife."

Relief and joy surged through me as I slipped the ring onto her finger. It fit perfectly, like it was meant to be. We both laughed, the sound a mix of tears and happiness.

I stood up and pulled her into my arms, holding her close as the reality of the moment sank in. We were engaged. We were going to spend the rest of our lives together.

As we pulled away, I cupped her face in my hands, brushing away her tears with my thumbs. "I love you, Chloe," I murmured, leaning in to kiss her. Our lips met in a tender, lingering kiss, the world around us fading away. It was a kiss filled with promise, with the certainty of a shared future.

When we finally broke apart, Chloe was smiling, her eyes shining with love and happiness. "I love you too," she said, her voice trembling with emotion. "More than words can ever express."

We sat there for a while longer, wrapped in each other's arms, watching the sun dip below the horizon. The sky darkened, stars beginning to twinkle in the night sky.

It felt like the beginning of a new chapter, a new adventure. We talked about our future, about our plans for a small, intimate wedding with our closest friends and the people we've helped.

We imagined a life filled with love, laughter, and new beginnings.

As the night grew colder, we gathered our things and made our way back to the inn. The village was quiet, the streets empty save for a few wandering tourists.

We walked hand in hand, our hearts full of love and excitement. There was a sense of peace in the air, a feeling that everything was as it should be.

Back in our room, we snuggled under the covers, the warmth of each other's presence a comforting balm.

As we drifted off to sleep, I couldn't help but feel grateful for the journey that had brought us here. It hadn't been easy, but it had been worth it.

And now, as we faced a future filled with hope and possibilities, I knew that there was no one else I'd rather spend it with.

Chloe was my partner, my confidante, my love. She was my everything. And as I held her close, I knew that no matter what challenges lay ahead, we would face them together.

Because together, we were unstoppable. Together, we were home.

19

Chloe

The coastal town where we decided to exchange our vows felt like something out of a dream. Nestled between rolling hills and the sparkling blue sea, it had an air of timelessness, as if it existed in a world untouched by the chaos of the outside.

The morning sun bathed everything in a golden hue, and the scent of saltwater mixed with blooming jasmine filled the air. It was the perfect setting for our wedding—a simple, intimate affair, just as we wanted.

As I stood in front of the mirror in our quaint little suite, I felt a mixture of excitement and nerves. My dress was a delicate ivory lace, flowing and ethereal, with intricate embroidery that danced along the hem.

My hair, styled in loose waves, was adorned with small white flowers, and my makeup was soft and natural. I felt beautiful, but more importantly, I felt like myself. Today wasn't about grandeur or spectacle; it was about celebrating the love Adrian and I had fought so hard to protect.

A knock on the door pulled me from my thoughts. "Come in," I called, my voice trembling with anticipation.

The door creaked open, and there stood Adrian, looking devastatingly handsome in a tailored navy suit. His eyes widened slightly as he took me in, a slow smile spreading across his face. "You look stunning," he said, his voice husky with emotion.

I felt a blush creep up my cheeks. "You don't look so bad yourself," I teased, stepping closer to him.

He reached out, gently tracing the outline of my jaw with his fingers. "Are you ready?" he asked, his eyes searching mine.

I nodded, my heart swelling with love and certainty. "I've never been more ready for anything in my life."

We made our way to the small chapel by the sea, where our closest friends and the people we had helped along the way awaited us. The ceremony was held outdoors, with a breathtaking view of the ocean as our backdrop.

The sound of waves crashing against the shore provided a natural symphony, and the gentle breeze carried the soft melodies of a violinist playing in the background.

As I walked down the aisle, arm in arm with my dear friend Lena, my heart pounded in my chest. The guests stood, smiling warmly at me, their eyes filled with joy and support. At the end of the aisle, Adrian waited, his gaze locked on mine. The love in his eyes was palpable, and it gave me the strength to take each step with confidence.

When I finally reached him, Lena handed me over, giving me a quick, encouraging squeeze. Adrian took my hands in his, and we turned to face each other, the world around us fading away.

The officiant began to speak, but all I could focus on was Adrian—the way his eyes sparkled with unshed tears, the slight tremor in his hands, the way he looked at me like I was the only person in the world.

We exchanged vows, each word carrying the weight of our shared past and the promise of our future. Adrian spoke first, his voice steady but filled with emotion.

"Chloe, you are my light, my strength, my home. We've been through so much together, and every moment has only made me love you more. I promise to stand by you, to support you, and to love you for the rest of our lives. You are my heart, my soul, my everything."

Tears welled in my eyes as I spoke my vows, my voice trembling with the depth of my feelings. "Adrian, you've shown me what it means to love and be loved unconditionally. You've been my anchor, my protector, my partner. I promise to cherish you, to stand beside you, and to love you with all that I am. You are my safe haven, my greatest adventure, my forever."

The officiant pronounced us husband and wife, and Adrian leaned in, capturing my lips in a tender kiss.

 The guests erupted into applause, but all I could feel was the warmth of his embrace and the softness of his lips. It was a kiss filled with love, passion, and the promise of a lifetime together.

The reception was a joyous affair, filled with laughter, dancing, and heartfelt speeches. We dined on exquisite local cuisine, and the wine flowed freely.

The atmosphere was one of celebration and love, and for the first time in years, I felt a sense of peace and belonging.
This was our new beginning, a fresh start

surrounded by the people who mattered most to us.

As the night drew to a close, Adrian and I slipped away from the festivities, making our way to a secluded spot by the beach.

The moon hung high in the sky, casting a silver glow over the water. We kicked off our shoes and walked along the shore, the cool sand beneath our feet and the gentle waves licking at our ankles.

Adrian pulled me into his arms, and we swayed together, the sound of the ocean our only music. He kissed me softly, his lips gentle and loving. "Thank you for making me the happiest man alive," he whispered, his voice filled with emotion.

I smiled, feeling a warmth spread through me. "Thank you for being my partner," I replied, my heart swelling with love.

We continued to dance under the stars, lost in each other's embrace. The world felt right, and for the first time in a long time, I felt truly at peace.

 As we made our way back to our suite, hand in hand, I knew that this was just the beginning of our journey.

We had faced our past, conquered our demons, and found each other. And now, as husband and wife, we were ready to face whatever the future held, together.

In the privacy of our room, we celebrated our union in a way only we could. The night was filled with passion, tenderness, and the kind of intimacy that only comes from truly knowing and loving someone.

As we lay tangled together, basking in the afterglow, I couldn't help but marvel at the journey that had brought us here.

Adrian held me close, his fingers gently tracing patterns on my skin. "I can't believe you're mine," he murmured, his voice thick with love.

I smiled, feeling a deep sense of contentment. "You, me, us, this moment itself proves that we are together for love" I replied, snuggling closer to him.

As we drifted off to sleep, wrapped in each other's arms, we were together, we were unstoppable. Together, we were home.

20

Chloe

Life had a way of surprising me, often when I least expected it. Standing in my office at Bennet Securities, I marvelled at the twists and turns that had brought me here. The office was sleek and modern, a perfect blend of Adrian's sharp aesthetic and my penchant for comfort.

 I glanced at the framed photos on my desk—snapshots of our wedding, our travels, and the people we'd helped along the way. Each image was a reminder of the life we'd built together, a life far removed from the chaos of our past.

As the Director of Client Services, my role was both challenging and rewarding. I spent my days coordinating with clients, managing projects, and ensuring our team had everything they needed to succeed. It was fulfilling work, especially knowing that our company was making a real difference in the world.

Bennet Securities had become a beacon of hope for victims of trafficking and other social injustices, and I was proud to be a part of it.

Just as I was about to dive into a mountain of paperwork, my office door swung open, and Adrian strolled in. He looked every bit the confident CEO, dressed in a tailored suit that emphasized his broad shoulders and lean frame. His smile was mischievous, and I could tell he was up to something.

"What's with the grin?" I asked, raising an eyebrow.

He leaned against my desk, crossing his arms over his chest. "Oh, nothing," he said nonchalantly, "just thinking about how much I love surprising my wife."

I narrowed my eyes playfully. "What did you do, Adrian?"

He pulled a small envelope from his pocket and handed it to me. I opened it cautiously, revealing two tickets to a tropical island getaway. My eyes widened in surprise. "You planned a vacation?"

He nodded, his grin widening. "I figured we could use a break. Sun, sand, and no work for a whole week. What do you say?"

I laughed, feeling a rush of excitement. "I say you're the best husband ever." I stood up and wrapped my arms around his neck, pulling him in for a kiss. His lips were warm and familiar, and I felt a flutter of happiness in my chest.

"You're amazing, you know that?" I whispered against his lips.

He chuckled, his hands resting on my waist. "of course, thanks to my love of life" he replied, his voice low and teasing.

We pulled away, and I couldn't help but giggle. "So, when do we leave?"

"Tomorrow," he said, winking. "Just enough time to wrap up our work and pack."

I sighed, shaking my head. "You really thought of everything, didn't you?"

"Of course," he said, his tone mock-serious. "I take my role as husband very sincerely."

I laughed again, feeling a lightness in my heart. This was what our life had become—a beautiful blend of work and play, challenges and triumphs. And I wouldn't have it any other way.

Adrian

Watching Chloe's face light up when she saw the tickets was priceless. It was moments like these that made everything worth it—the long hours, the tough decisions, the constant balancing act of work and personal life. Seeing her smile, knowing I could make her happy, filled me with a deep sense of satisfaction.

As the CEO of Bonnet Securities, my days were packed with meetings, strategy sessions, and the occasional crisis management. But the work was fulfilling, a far cry from the shadowy world of espionage I had once known. Here, I was building something tangible, something good. And I had Chloe by my side, her passion and drive matching my own.

The next day, we wrapped up our work and boarded a flight to our tropical paradise. The journey was filled with laughter and playful banter, a welcome escape from the usual grind. As we stepped off the plane, the warm, humid air enveloped us, and I felt an instant sense of relaxation. The island was a picture-perfect getaway, with pristine beaches, crystal-clear waters, and lush greenery.

We checked into our beachfront villa, and Chloe's eyes sparkled with excitement as she took in the stunning view. "This is incredible," she breathed, turning to me with a wide smile.

I grinned, feeling a surge of pride. "Only the best for you, my love."

We spent the next few days soaking up the sun, exploring the island, and indulging in delicious local cuisine. We swam in the ocean, lounged by the pool, and even tried our hand at snorkelling, which resulted in some hilarious moments.

Chloe, ever the adventurer, was eager to explore the underwater world, while I struggled to keep up. As Ex-M16 agent I am good on land stuff and water is like I can swim for survival but underwater play... At one point, I accidentally swallowed a mouthful of saltwater, sputtering and coughing as Chloe doubled over with laughter.

"Are you okay?" she asked, still giggling.

I nodded, grinning despite the discomfort. "Yeah, yeah, I'm fine. Just not used to breathing underwater, apparently."

She shook her head, her eyes shining with amusement. "You're hopeless," she teased, but her tone was affectionate.

Back at our villa, we lounged on the deck, sipping on fruity cocktails as the sun set over the horizon. The sky was a riot of colours, casting a warm glow over everything. Chloe leaned her head on my shoulder, and I wrapped my arm around her, pulling her close.

"This is perfect," she murmured, her voice soft and content.

I kissed the top of her head, feeling a wave of love wash over me. "It really is," I agreed. "You know, I never thought I'd find this kind of peace."

She looked up at me, her eyes full of love and understanding. "Me neither," she admitted. "But I'm glad we did. We deserve this, Adrian. We've been through so much, and we came out stronger because of it."

I nodded, feeling a lump in my throat. "You're right. We do deserve this."

We sat in comfortable silence for a while, watching the sun disappear below the horizon. As the stars began to twinkle in the night sky, I turned to Chloe, my heart full of gratitude and love.

"You know," I began, my voice low, "I never imagined my life could be this good. You brought so much light into my world, Chloe. You've given me hope, joy, and a sense of purpose. I can't thank you enough for that."

She smiled, her eyes soft and warm. "You've done the same for me, Adrian. I love you, and I can't wait to see what the future holds for us."

I leaned in and kissed her, slow and tender, pouring all my love and gratitude into that kiss. It was a kiss full of promise, a reminder of the beautiful life we were building together. As we pulled away, I rested my forehead against hers, feeling a sense of peace settle over me.

"We're going to be best couple" I whispered, my voice filled with conviction.

She nodded, a serene smile on her lips. "Yes, we are."

And in that moment, I knew that no matter what challenges lay ahead, we would face them together. Because together, we were stronger, braver, and happier. Together, we had found our place in the world, and it was exactly where we were meant to be.

Epilogue

Chloe

Two years had passed, and as I stood on the cliff overlooking the sea, I felt a profound sense of peace wash over me. The wind rustled through my hair, and I placed a hand on my slightly swollen belly, feeling the gentle flutter of life within me.

It was hard to believe how much had changed since that fateful day when Adrian and I decided to leave our tumultuous pasts behind and build a future together. Now, we were not just partners in life and work but also on the cusp of becoming parents.

Adrian stood beside me; his hand intertwined with mine. The sun was setting, casting a golden glow over the horizon, painting the sky in hues of orange and pink. It was a sight that never failed to take my breath away, a reminder of the beauty in the world despite the darkness we'd faced.

I turned to Adrian, "Can you believe it?" I asked, my voice soft and full of wonder. "We're going to be parents."

Adrian smiled, his eyes crinkling at the corners. "I know," he said, squeezing my hand gently. "It's surreal, isn't it? But in the best possible way."

We stood in comfortable silence, reflecting on the journey that had brought us here. Our work at Bennet Securities had flourished, and we'd helped countless people rebuild their lives.

It was fulfilling work, but we'd also learned to balance it with the simple joys of everyday life. We took time for ourselves, whether it was a quiet dinner at home, a spontaneous trip, or simply a lazy afternoon spent reading and cuddling on the couch.

Suddenly, a playful thought crossed my mind, and I grinned mischievously. " Do you remember your first time cooking for me after we learned about my pregnancy?" I teased, nudging him lightly. "You nearly burned down the kitchen."

Adrian chuckled, shaking his head. "Hey, in my defence, I thought more olive oil would make the dish taste better."

I laughed, the sound light and carefree. "It tasted like an oil spill," I teased, giggling at the memory. "But it was sweet of you to try."

Adrian rolled his eyes good-naturedly. "I still maintain that my grilled cheese is top-notch," he said, feigning indignation.

I raised an eyebrow, smirking. "Sure, if you like it extra crispy."

We both laughed, the sound mingling with the crashing waves below. It was moments like these that reminded me of how lucky we were—how far we'd come from the shadows of our past. Our love had been tested in ways we couldn't have imagined, but we'd come out stronger, more resilient, and deeply in love.

As the sun dipped below the horizon, I felt a sense of contentment settle over me. I leaned into Adrian, resting my head on his shoulder. "Do you ever think about the future?" I asked, my voice barely above a whisper.

Adrian turned to me, his eyes soft and thoughtful. "All the time," he admitted. "I think about our child, about the life we're going to give them. I think about us, growing old together, still teasing each other over burned dinners and bad jokes."

I smiled, feeling a warmth spread through me. "That sounds perfect," I said, my heart full.

***

Adrian

Standing on the cliff, with Chloe's head resting on my shoulder, I felt a deep sense of fulfilment. The journey we'd taken to get here had been anything but easy, but looking at the woman beside me, I knew every step had been worth it.

Chloe was my anchor, my partner, my everything. And now, she is

 mother of our unborn child. It was a thought that filled me with awe and a touch of nervous excitement.

The sun had set, and the first stars began to twinkle in the night sky. It was a beautiful night, and I couldn't help but think back to all the nights we'd spent on this very cliff, talking about our dreams and fears, our hopes for the future. Now, those dreams were becoming a reality.

I glanced down at Chloe, a playful smile tugging at my lips. "Do you remember that time we got lost in the Italian countryside?" I asked, my tone teasing. "You were so adamant about not using the GPS."

Chloe chuckled, her eyes twinkling with amusement. "Hey, I thought it would be more romantic to navigate by the stars," she defended, grinning.

I shook my head, laughing. "We ended up in a cow field," I reminded her, unable to keep the laughter out of my voice. "And you were convinced the cows were judging us."

Chloe giggled, the sound light and melodious. "They totally were," she insisted, giggling. "I've never seen cows look so unimpressed."

I smiled, leaning down to kiss her softly. The kiss was tender, a reminder of the love we shared and the life we were building together. As we pulled away, I looked into her eyes, feeling a swell of emotion.

"Chloe," I began, my voice steady, "I want you to know that no matter what happens, I'll always be here for you. For us. For our family. We've been through so much, and we've come out stronger. I know we'll face whatever comes next together."

Chloe smiled, her eyes glistening with unshed tears. "I know," she whispered, her voice filled with love. "And I feel the same way."

We stood there, hand in hand, staring out at the vast ocean. The stars above seemed to shine brighter, as if blessing us with their light. In that moment, I felt an overwhelming sense of peace. We were finally free from the shadows of our past, and our future was full of possibilities.

As we turned to head back to our car, Chloe suddenly stopped, a mischievous glint in her eye. "You know," she said, her tone playful, "we never did finish that dance lesson."

I raised an eyebrow, intrigued. "Oh? Are you challenging me to a dance-off?"

Chloe grinned, nodding. "You're on," she said, her voice filled with excitement.

Laughing, I pulled her into my arms, and we began to dance under the starlit sky. It was a spontaneous, silly moment, full of twirls and laughter. Chloe's laughter rang out, and I couldn't help but join in. We danced like no one was watching, like we were the only two people in the world.

As the night wore on, we finally slowed down, catching our breath. I looked at Chloe, her cheeks flushed and her eyes sparkling with joy. "I love you," I whispered, feeling the truth of those words deep in my soul.

Chloe smiled, her eyes shining with love. "I love you too," she replied, her voice soft and tender.

And in that moment, I knew that no matter what the future held, we would face it together, with love and laughter. Our journey had been long and challenging, but it had brought us to this place of peace and happiness. And as we stood there, holding each other under the starlit sky,

 I knew that our legacy was not just in the lives we'd saved, but in the love we'd found. It was a love that would continue to guide us, a love that would light our way, even in the darkest of times.

In a perilous game of captor and captive.
They shouldn't have met...but they did.
He shouldn't want her...but
he's keeping her anyway.

Read Elite Hearts – Vows of Vengeance

Dive into the steamy and forbidden romance of
Marco and Yumi.

Turn the page for an exclusive glimpse...

For availability updates check on
https://sites.google.com/view/aditi-j-writes/home

Vows of Vengeance

ELITE HEARTS SERIES

BOOK 1

1

YUMI

I had finally done it. Graduating at the top of my class as a nurse wasn't just an accomplishment— it felt like the closing of one long, carefully planned chapter of my life.

I could almost hear my mother's voice in the back of my head, reminding me that I was now ready to start a career far away from my father's shadow. That was her plan all along, wasn't it? To shape me into someone who had no ties to the man who once ruled our lives.

But today, I didn't want to think about that. Not my father, not my mother, not the tangled mess of my family's past. Today was supposed to be mine.

The sun glistened on the calm waters of Lake Geneva as I stepped out of the auditorium, the soft breeze carrying the scent of fresh flowers from the graduation ceremony.

Montreux looked so beautiful in the early summer—peaceful, almost like it was untouched by the rest of the world's problems. That was why I loved it here. It felt... safe. Separate. A world away from the chaos of Japan and everything I'd left behind.

I took a deep breath and walked toward the promenade; the click of my heels barely audible over the gentle hum of life around me. Tourists filled the cafés, couples strolled hand in hand, and a few boats rocked lazily in the water. For a moment, I let myself imagine that this was all my life could be from now on—simple, peaceful. A life I had built for myself.

But reality had a way of intruding, even on days like this. A familiar buzz vibrated against my palm. My phone. I already knew who it would be before I even glanced at the screen.

Mom.

I sighed, my fingers hovering over the 'decline' button. I didn't want to talk to her right now. Not on today of all days. But avoiding her wasn't going to make her stop.

With another deep breath, I swiped the call open.

"Yumi, darling," she greeted me in her usual clipped tone, the one that left no room for excuses or disagreement. "Congratulations on your graduation."

I could hear her smile through the phone, but it felt more like the cold kind of pride she always had—because I'd done what she wanted, not necessarily what I wanted. "Thanks, Mom," I replied, my voice polite, but distant.

"Have you thought about when you'll be coming back to Nagoya?" she asked, already steering the conversation toward her plans for me. "I've arranged a few interviews for you at the hospital here. It's important to get started quickly, Yumi. You don't want to waste time."

I bit the inside of my cheek, staring out over the lake. "Actually, I was thinking of staying in Montreux for a little while. Just for a week or so. I need some time to unwind before I come back."

"Unwind?" Her voice sharpened, laced with disapproval. "You've been away long enough. It's time to focus on your career, on your future. You know how important this is, Yumi."

She always made it sound like I'd disappear into the world of the Yakuza if I stayed away from her too long. I knew she was just afraid. She'd never say it, but she feared I'd be dragged into my father's orbit, into that dark underworld she had fought so hard to escape.

But that wasn't me. I wasn't some puppet waiting to be pulled into the violence and power struggles of my father's world. I'd made my own choices, built my own life—one that had nothing to do with him.

And while my mother feared and hated him for everything he was, I didn't feel the same. I didn't hate my father. In fact, we still spoke from time to time, his calls often surprising me late at night, his deep voice calm and steady. There was something about those conversations that always left me feeling... conflicted. He wasn't the monster my mother made him out to be.

We weren't close, not really. But I didn't fear him like she did.

"I just need a little more time, Mom," I said, forcing my voice to stay even. "I'll come back soon; I promise."

There was a long pause on the other end of the line. "Fine," she finally said, her tone still stiff. "But don't take too long, Yumi. You have responsibilities now. It's time to start thinking seriously about your future."

"I will."

She ended the call before I could say anything else.

I slipped my phone back into my bag and let out a heavy sigh. That was my mother. Always controlling, always pushing me in the direction she thought was right. It wasn't like I didn't appreciate what she'd done for me—raising me on her own after the divorce, protecting me from the dangerous world my father ruled. But sometimes it felt like I was living a life that wasn't fully mine.

I glanced at the horizon, where the lake met the sky in soft blues and golds. For now, this was my life. This week was mine. One week to breathe, to think, to decide what I wanted next. I wasn't in any rush to go back to Japan, to Nagoya, or to the suffocating expectations that waited for me there.

I made my way down to the water's edge, slipping off my heels and letting my toes sink into the cool grass. I couldn't remember the last time I felt this free, without the weight of someone else's expectations pressing down on me.

But that freedom felt fragile, like it could be taken away at any moment. Even though I was far from Japan, far from my father and the world he lived in, there was always a part of me that wondered if I'd ever really be able to escape it.

My mother had tried so hard to make sure I stayed away from him; from everything he represented. But blood ties were complicated. They pulled at you in ways you didn't always expect.

For now, though, I wasn't going to think about that. I wasn't going to think about the life waiting for me in Japan, or the shadow of my father that I could never quite shake.

Today, I would just be Yumi Asano—the girl who had worked hard, who had made it through years of study, and who deserved a break.

Tomorrow could wait.

2

MARCO

The world is full of people who don't know when they've crossed the line. My job has always been to remind them. But Hiroshi Asano—he didn't just cross the line. He shattered it.

I watch from the car as Yumi Asano walks along the promenade in Geneva, her steps light, her expression calm and relaxed.

She looks like she doesn't have a care in the world. She's innocent in all of this. And yet,

she's everything I need to finish what started all those years ago.

My grip tightens around the glass in my hand, and the ice cubes clink against the sides.

 The view is stunning—this postcard-perfect lakefront, the mountains, the peacefulness—but it feels like nothing more than a backdrop to the chaos brewing inside me. Chaos I've controlled for years, waiting for the right moment to strike.

Yumi is the last piece of this puzzle. Hiroshi Asano's only daughter. Untouchable, at least until now.

...

***

Keen to dive deeper into Yumi and Marco's steamy story?

Get **Vows of Vengeance**, the first book in the steamy romance series **Elite Hearts**.

Grateful to all my readers for embracing
Shadows of the Heart.

With my love for this book and the upcoming
ones, I would be even more grateful if you could
share your reviews on the platforms of your
choice.

With love,

Aditi

Want to discuss my books and share your
dreamiest romantic moments with fellow
romance readers?
Reach me on Instagram at
_aditi.j.writes
and get connected with like-minded romantic and
reverie-filled readers by joining
A.J's Elite Hearts

<u>**Elite Hearts**</u>
An interconnected standalone book series.

Vows of Vengeance

To easily access all of my books:
https://sites.google.com/view/aditi-j-writes/home

About the Author

Aditi.J is a steamy new adult and contemporary romance author. Her stories are filled with dynamic characters, from alphas to those in both light and dark romantic settings. Her characters are always swoonworthy, capturing hearts with every page.

Outside of reading and writing, Aditi is a green tea lover and nature enthusiast, often lost in reverie over fictional male leads and their captivating stories.